NOWHERE TO RUN

NJ MOSS

First published in 2024 by Bloodhound Books.

www.bloodhoundbooks.com

Print ISBN: 978-1-916978-60-7

1

KATY

"You did really well today," Joel tells me, as I sit in a heap of sweat trying to remember how to breathe. I try to smile up at him, but my eyes are stinging. I wipe myself with the towel again. He chuckles. "Seriously, Katy. I think it'll be time for your blue belt soon."

"I'm just happy I'm making progress." I sound like a cat on the verge of vomiting. "It doesn't always feel like that."

Joel squats deep with stunning flexibility. I've been doing Brazilian jujitsu for almost two years. It's a form of grappling – basically grabbing each other, rolling around on the floor, and trying to choke, or snap an arm, or crush a bicep. It's fun… and I'm *slightly* tougher than when I started. Joel is ten years younger than me – oh, to be twenty-two again. "I mean it. Just surviving on the ground, with a big, violent man on top of you… being able to break his posture and stop him from inflicting *mental* damage. That's an achievement."

"I'm still waiting for you to teach me a magic move that will let me defeat anyone, no matter the size."

He grins tightly. "That's for the films, I'm afraid. You know what I say…"

"The best defence will always be a one-hundred-metre sprint."

"Bingo."

I stand up, rolling my shoulders. Every Thursday after class, I feel like I've been through a war. Even when I can tell that the higher grades – I'm still a white belt – are going easy on me, it's still tough. But it's better than thinking about what will happen when somebody's on top of me and I have no idea what to do. No defences. And then… but I made a promise to myself not to be so depressing. No more thinking about the *and thens* of life.

"Thank you, professor," I tell Joel.

He chuckles, rolling his eyes. "How many times do I have to tell you, you don't have to call me that?"

"At least one more," I reply, like I always do.

The sense of routine and habit feels good. Every Thursday, I wipe myself down and then wait outside for my taxi. Once upon a time Katy Mitchell would've driven here, hopped back in the car, no thought of panic attacks, no thought of losing control. But I'm too distrustful now – of myself. Maybe that's pathetic. But screw it. I like the cool winter air, like leaning against the lamppost, humming a tune while I wait. It's the same every week. When I get home, I'll put on a podcast, run a warm bath, maybe order a takeaway.

My mobile rings. It's Mum. "Are you done with kung fu class, then?"

I laugh. "Hello to you too."

"Your father wants to know, roast chicken or lasagna tomorrow?"

My life has become much simpler since The Incident: the thing that made me start taking Brazilian jujitsu to begin with. I'm sure you can figure it out. A woman blocks something out. A woman doesn't want to think about it. A woman can't even address it in her own mind. Most people would arrive at the same conclusion. If I explicitly address it, even in my own head, it twists me up. Not as much as it used to, though, so that's something.

"Chicken would be nice," I say.

"Chicken it is, then," Mum replies. "How was class tonight, anyway?"

"Oh, you know, just a complete waste of time."

Mum tuts. "I never said a *complete* waste of time. It's just, really, dear… I don't want you to get a false idea of what you're capable of."

There are some mothers who would mean this in a spiteful way. Through my work as a counsellor, I've seen the vicious effects bad mother–daughter dynamics can have. But I know Mum's coming from a good place. She's just worried about me.

"I'm not at some bullshido self-defence class."

"Bull-whatto?"

"It's what people call bullshit martial arts. Bullshido."

"Do you *really* have to curse?"

"You asked. The point is, I'm very aware of my limitations. Believe me. Far more than I was before."

"Well – that's good."

Before The Incident, I'd spent eight years in a self-defence school. We never sparred each other, never actually practised fighting. We'd go through a lot of choreographed moves. If Person A grabs you here, perform Action B. The problem came when Person A grabbed me, I did Action B… and then he just kept going. I was lost. I shut down mentally. All that training – I was almost a black belt in this nonsense system – amounted to nothing.

Now: Brazilian jujitsu, and sometimes the boxing class on Saturday afternoons, depending on how high my workload is. Counselling others is far easier than handling my own mind.

"Katy?" Mum says, jarring me to the present moment.

"Yeah?"

"I said… I love you and I'll see you tomorrow. Be safe."

"I will," I reply. "I love you too."

After hanging up, a taxi pulls into the industrial estate. It's dark now, my breath fogging. Maybe I'll order a pizza from the place that does the stuffed crust. I'm trying to keep to a fairly strict diet, mostly because it seems to help with my mood. But after my Thursday night class, I'm always so exhausted and achy, greedily devouring an entire family-size pizza is just heaven.

The taxi comes to a stop. It's got the same *Orange Taxis* sign on the door. It has the glowing taxi light on the roof. I'm not great with cars, but it looks like the same make and model as the other Orange Taxis: the main taxi service in Weston-super-Mare.

I climb into the backseat. The driver is a man I don't recognise, but that's not unusual. Even so, I have to internally warn myself not to be a complete psycho: warn myself not to let my thoughts sprint off into paranoia land. He's tall, hunching over so he doesn't touch the roof. Wide shoulders. Handsome in a vague way that doesn't rely on any specific features.

"Ten Baytree Road, love?" he says.

"Yes, please."

"All right-ee, then. Saddle up."

He laughs as if this is supposed to be a joke. So I laugh with him. But secretly I hope he's not going to be one of those chatty drivers. I do so much talking in my work, sometimes I become a happy loner during my out-of-work hours. My friend Trish often jokes I'm ready to be a pensioner already.

The man glances in the rear-view before he turns away. Strangely, it's only now that I notice the glass. There's a glass divider between the front of the car and the back, with small holes allowing us to speak. This isn't unusual in taxis generally speaking, but I've never seen it in a local one.

"I meant, put your seat belt on, darling."

"Oh, right." When he calls me *darling* – and when I hurriedly follow his instructions – I'm reminded of before. The Incident. The pain. Both physical and emotional. "Okay, done."

"Top marks," he says.

"Is this new?" I ask, gesturing to the glass.

"Yeah, rolling out in all the cars soon. Too many problems on Friday and Saturday nights. But you won't be giving me any problems, will you, Katy?"

For a second, the far-too-prickly part of my mind flares up. *How does he know my name?* But, obviously, he knows it because I've used this same taxi service every Thursday for the past two years. I need to relax.

"Makes sense," I say.

He starts driving, turning out of the industrial estate and toward the dual carriageway. It should only take around ten or fifteen minutes to get home. Then… bath, food, isolation. Bliss.

"You doing boxing in there, were you?" the man asks after a minute or so.

"Jujitsu," I tell him.

"What's that, then? Rolling around on the floor?"

"Pretty much," I say. "It's a grappling martial art. Taking each other down. Trying to get chokes, submissions, stuff like that."

"Black belt, are you?"

I wonder if I'm imagining his slightly condescending tone. When I was a student at a bullshido school – when I truly believed, in my heart of hearts, I was tougher than most people – I used to console myself when people talked down to me. I used to think, *I could kick their arse if I wanted.* Now, humbled and thankfully still alive, I understand how insane that is. Even with two years of grappling and boxing experience, this man would be a serious problem for me.

"No," I say, then look out the window, hoping he gets the point.

"Hang on. I've heard of it, I think. It's all about the smaller person being able to twist up the bigger bloke like he's a pretzel, ain't it?"

"Not really," I murmur, a prickle moving up my spine. But there's nothing new there. I was in the supermarket last week and flinched when a big man brushed by me with his trolley.

"Hmm, that's what I heard. Reckon you could take me, darling?"

I wish I had the social confidence, or self-respect, or whatever it is, to tell him I'd rather continue the journey in silence. But it's far easier to advise somebody to do that than do it myself.

"I don't think so," I tell him. "I just hope I never have to find out."

I've never thought of laughter as a weapon before, but his is somehow aggressive. "Yeah, me too. For *my* sake, obviously."

When he drives down the dual carriageway, getting further from town and closer to the outskirts of Weston-super-Mare, I let myself imagine I'm in the bubble bath. I like to turn off all the lights and sink into the water, let whatever podcast I'm listening to completely take over my thoughts.

My phone vibrates. I take it out, expecting a text from Mum. But it's a notification from the Orange Taxis application.

Your driver has arrived.

More paranoia grips me. Why am I only getting this notification now?

What's more likely… the application is running slow, or this taxi isn't a real taxi?

"Everything all right?" the driver says. "You look like you've just had some bad news."

"It's…" *It's just that the Orange Taxis app has just informed me the driver has arrived, but I'm already in your car, which means you're not the driver. Which means something very bad is happening here.*

I can't say any of that. I'd sound insane. Maybe I *am*, on some level. But I'd like to keep that to myself. "Nothing," I finish. "I'm fine."

"Okee-dokee," he says in a forced cheery tone. "We'll get you where you belong in no time at all, Katy. Don't fret."

I nod, look out the window. We're driving past the same fields I pass every Thursday. The same supermarket. The same bus stop with one broken pane in the plastic. And yet there's an alarm screeching inside of me, as if something terrible is going to happen. My nervous system is far too prone to fight-or-flight. Martial arts is helping, but even after two years, it's still difficult to calm myself down.

That's fine. Not long now. Then I'll be home. There's no need to be dramatic about it.

2

KATY

A minute later, my phone vibrates again. The Orange Taxis app lets the drivers message the passengers. I've got a new message. It's from Ravi, a driver who's picked me up many times before.

Hello Miss Mitchell, where are you? I am here.

The driver – the regular-looking man sitting on the other side of the glass – is humming a tune as he turns into the residential area where I live. It's near the exit to the motorway, but tucked away from the main flow of traffic. It's useful for when I travel to my Bristol office, though I work from home a lot too. I type:

I think there's a mistake. I'm already in the taxi.

You are already in an Orange Taxi?

Yes.

That is very strange.

"Everything all right?" the driver asks.

Shamefully, this makes me flinch. *Flinch.* Just a simple question. Obviously, there's been a mix-up and the company has sent two cars. If I was counselling myself in this situation, I'd recommend staying calm and not leaping to conclusions.

"Uh, yes. I think so. It's my Orange Taxis app. Ravi is saying he's at the martial arts studio to pick me up."

"Ravi," the man says, as if the name makes him sick. "Yeah, I'm sure he's got himself good and confused. That's the second time this week he's tried to steal a fare."

What is the name of your driver, Miss Mitchell?

"What's your name?" I ask.

"Let me get to the bottom of this," the driver says, pulling up at the side of the road. It's so quiet. He parks in darkness, probably not on purpose, but it doesn't help the alarm wailing inside of me… the alarm I'm doing my best to stifle. The driver takes out his mobile, presses a few buttons, holds it to his ear. "All right, Shelley. Ravi's trying to snatch my fares again. No – I know. But he's messaging my current passenger on the app. Freaking her right out."

Is it that obvious?

Miss Mitchell?

Ravi sends, when I don't reply.

"Just thought I'd let you know," the driver goes on. "He needs to have some goddamned respect. Yeah, yeah. All right, lovely. See you in a bit."

He hangs up, then switches on the interior light. When he turns to me, I see he's not as regular as I thought. He's got two different coloured eyes, one blue and one green, and he has a crescent scar on his forehead. He smiles, making him seem younger. I guess he's around forty.

"Sorry about that," he says. "You can ignore Ravi. Bit of a rivalry going on, honestly."

"Oh. Sure." But I don't put my phone away. "Sorry – what was your name?"

"What *was* my name? Or what *is* my name?"

I'm familiar with this tactic, purposefully delaying the conversation. It's normally so one of my clients can give themselves room to think. Or lie. In a session, depending on the client, I might call them out for this. But there's something in the driver's mismatched eyes that stops me.

"What is your name?" I ask.

A moment of hesitation. His smile falters – then it's back, leaving me to wonder if I imagined the slip. We're so close to my flat. A few more minutes then I'll be listening to a podcast about counselling or jujitsu or something historical. "Markus," he says. "That was and *is* my name. Ha!"

He turns away and pulls out of the parking spot.

His name is Markus.

I write to Ravi, wishing he was driving me instead. I wouldn't consider us friends, exactly, but we've had some laughs and shared some pleasant small talk. Plus, he's way more respectful than Markus.

Markus?

Ravi replies, as the car takes me closer and closer to my flat.

Yes, he just spoke to Shelley on the phone.

I won't mention what Markus said to Shelley, the whole stealing-his-fares thing.

"Is Ravi still giving you hassle?" Markus says.

"No. I'm texting a friend."

I'm not sure why I lie… except I do. It's that alarm: the one I'm doing my best to ignore.

"Not long now." He turns the car down the second to last street. Down to the end of this one, turn at the small pharmacy, then home. Then bath. Then peace. "Sorry about the mix-up."

"It's okay," I tell him. "A taxi's a taxi at the end of the day."

"Try telling that to Ravi," Markus says, shaking his head ruefully. "He thinks because he's worked here longer than me, he has first dibs on every single bloody fare. It's enough to make a man resentful, honestly."

The last thing I want is to get into a long, drawn-out quasi counselling conversation about this. My body is achy and sore from class. My mind is sore from all this overthinking.

My phone vibrates again. It's Ravi.

> Miss Mitchell… I do not have a colleague called Markus. Or Shelley.

3

KATY

This doesn't make any sense. Did Markus fake that phone call, then? And if this man is going to… oh, Christ. The heartbeat hammering is starting again. The useless and counterproductive tightness in my chest. The fist of nerves squeezing my gut. I take a long breath, force myself to acknowledge it. If Markus is going to *kidnap* me, then why is he taking me home? And how did he manage to steal an Orange Taxis taxi? And how did he know to pick me up at that precise time?

"You look like you've seen a ghost, Katy," the man says, with a glance, turning onto my street and slowing down. Slowing *way* down, to almost a walking pace. "I hope Ravi hasn't upset you."

"N-no." Goddamn stutter. It brings me back to my school days. "It's just…"

"Just? Come on. Don't make me guess." His mismatched eyes watch me in the rear-view. "I've never been very good at reading women."

"He said he doesn't know you. Or Shelley."

Markus' laugh is so convincing. It's a *here we go again, classic Ravi* laugh. It's the rueful chuckle of a man who's heard the same thing countless times. "That's Ravi for you. He can get pretty bitter and weird when he doesn't get his way."

"That doesn't sound like him."

"Course, *you're* not going to see that side of him, darling."

Finally, thankfully, the car pulls up outside my flat. Markus drums his fingers on the steering wheel, still watching me in the rear-view. "Don't make me ask, Katy," he says, with an unnerving grin.

Oh, he's talking about the money. "I've already paid through the app," I tell him.

"Really?" He shakes his head. "Fuck's sake. That money's gone straight to Ravi then. I'm sorry to do this, but with cost of living and everything, would you mind settling with me in cash? You'll be able to get a refund through the app."

Maybe that's all this is, a fare-stealing scam. I'm fine with that. I really just need to get into my flat, lock the door. Then, for next week, maybe I'll ring up Orange Taxis and specifically request Ravi. "Sure," I say. "How much is it?"

"Uh, call it a tenner."

It's actually seven pound fifty, but I take a ten-pound note from my purse, then gesture toward the glass. "I'll just pass it through the window." I reach for the door.

"No need," Markus says quickly. "There's a hatch. See that handle there? Right in the middle?"

I look over the plastic panelling. I can't see a handle or a lever or anything. "I'm sorry…"

"Come on, darling. You've got eyes, haven't you?"

That tightening in my chest and gut is getting way, way worse. "I must be having a slow day. I can't see it." I reach for the door, pull the handle. It's locked. I pull on it again. I'm beginning to shake now. When I talk, my voice comes out sounding raw and worried. "Can you open the door, please?"

"I'm afraid not," Markus says. "We've had too many fare

dodgers recently. I'd honestly be far more comfortable if you passed the money through the hatch."

"Can *you* open the hatch, then?"

He smirks at me in the rear-view. "You're a smart woman. You can figure it out."

I look over the panelling again. Finally, I see a tiny indentation. Reaching forward, I hook my finger into it and try to shift the hatch. But nothing happens. Markus laughs. "It looks like you're having fun with that thing."

"I'll leave the cash on the seat," I tell him.

"That's what this bloke said last night – then he snatched the notes and ran."

"Then *you* open the hatch!"

"Easy, Katy," Markus says in an infuriatingly calm tone. "We don't tolerate poor treatment of our drivers at Orange Taxis."

"What about poor treatment of your customers?" I snap. Honestly, I almost shout. I don't mean to. But the longer this goes on, the tenser I'm getting.

"It's not my intention to treat you poorly," Markus says, suddenly in customer-service mode. "Would you like to make a complaint?"

"I'd like to pay the fare and leave. Unlock the door, please."

"Katy—"

"Unlock the door *now*."

Markus turns, fiddles with the divider. A small panel folds outwards, allowing him to pass his hand through. I remember something Joel said a few weeks ago, after a particular difficult class. *Remember this level of intensity. Real violence happens quickly. It's awful. It's disgusting. But you have to get used to it. You have to understand that, if you ever need to truly defend yourself, you'll need to act brutally and decisively.*

So when Markus passes his hand through, I think about grabbing him, violently tugging… and then what? Am I going to be able to hold him in place? Probably not. And even if I could, what then? Cause enough pain to force him to unlock the door?

I hand him the ten-pound note. His touch is cold as he takes it, sending a sick shiver through me. I'm about to withdraw my hand when he tightens his grip. Time seems to slow. I hear the crinkling of the ten-pound note, feel his icy fingers wrapping around my hand. He holds tightly. I try pull my hand away… he holds me like it's easy. Like it's a joke.

"You knew what was happening the second you got into this car," he says. "I could tell. You knew. But you're too damn polite. Too awkward. Oh, Katy… you silly, silly girl."

4

HIM

Most people exist inside their regular, boring reality. There are a few – artists, travellers, entrepreneurs, criminals – who are aware that there's another layer to life. They know how evil the world can be; artists bleed this into their creations. They're accustomed to sudden, sometimes violent changes in the fabric of their world. But the *vast* majority are wilfully locked inside the nine-to-five, egg-and-chips, British-Bake-Off, *I saw the funniest thing in the newspaper last night* life. That makes it simpler for people like me. By the time somebody realises they're living inside an upside-down world, it's too late. Whatever I've decided to do has already happened.

I don't blame poor Katy for her lack of action. Reasonably speaking, from a purely animalistic and primal perspective, the moment that Ravi gentleman messaged her she should've gone berserk. She should've started hammering the windows, shattered them, stabbed me with a shard of glass if I tried to stop her. She could have rung the police. Something, anything except wasting time wondering if this was real.

But again, I can't blame her. It would be unreasonable to expect her to assume a handsome psychopath had decided to create a fake Orange Taxis taxi. She never would've guessed that I'd been watching her to get a good idea of her schedule: that I'd pinpointed her Thursday night martial arts class as the perfect opportunity to take her. It was simple enough to buy a second-hand car, install this protective glass, order the exact same signage. The rest was classic make-believe, *all right, love*, playing the stereotypical driver.

Now Katy Mitchell is in the worst position of her life. She's locked in my car. She has no idea what my intentions are. Hell, she doesn't even know *who* I am. But I know who I am. I know what I am. I'm a person who, when I decide to do something, acts decisively. I don't hesitate. And I don't care: in the practical sense. I don't feel like other people seem to. I want things – I have objectives – but I'd never waste time crying, hyperventilating, rendering myself pathetic.

I wonder if she has any idea why I've targeted her. But that's something else I have in my favour. Most people's motivations are similar. Family, money, sex, desire for material possessions. Mine are unique. I'm not special. I'll be worm food just like everybody else. Just like Katy. But while I'm here, I'm going to right a few wrongs.

Tonight's the night. I've been looking forward to it for months. The look of pure dread on Katy's face was worth the wait.

5

KATY

I snatch my hand away, pointlessly reach for the door handle. It's locked, obviously, so that does nothing. Markus – if that's his name – starts to laugh when I hammer at the window with my fist. The car screeches as he pulls out of the spot, quickly U-turns, and then surges back in the direction we've just come from.

I keep hitting the window, my hand pulsing with pain.

"It's reinforced glass," Markus says jovially. He sounds like he's loving this, the freak.

I quickly take out my phone again, click *emergency*. Markus sighs. "Fifty-four Puttingthorpe Drive," he says. It's my parents' address. "I'd take out your dad first. I saw you and him at a café a couple of weeks ago. He was walking with a cane. When you were in the bathroom, he kept wincing and touching his knee. So, first, I'd kick him over and over in that knee. And once he was crippled, I'd stamp on his face. Then I'd do very, very, very bad things to your mother while he was forced to watch."

Staring down at my phone, my vision starts to blur. Panic is trying to choke me. Markus is driving faster now. He's heading for the motorway… and then where?

"Go ahead," he says. "Ring the police. Tell them what's

happening. Maybe they'll be able to get to me before I can get to your parents. Or maybe, like they always do, the police will hesitate. They'll give me the time I need. Either way, I'm going to hurt somebody."

I move my thumb to the *call* button.

"Let's do it like this," Markus says. "You have five seconds to throw your phone out the window. Otherwise, I stop the car and kill you. Then I pay your parents a visit. Tonight's a special occasion. I'd prefer not to rush things. But, truthfully, I quite like the idea of killing you."

His tone doesn't change at all. It's just as difficult to take him seriously as it is to doubt his words. I'm aware that doesn't make much sense. It's like when one of my clients tries to explain some deep, primal feeling and it comes out as a barrage of barely connected words. Markus is either so cold he's a psycho. Or he's pretending to be one. But seeing as we've just joined motorway traffic and we're speeding away from Weston, I'm guessing he *is* genuine.

"Five," he says. "Four, three…"

He helpfully lowers the window for me. Wind rushes in. We must be going at least sixty.

"Two…" Suddenly, he slams his hand on the horn. I leap, seat belt cutting into me, dropping my phone in my lap. "Do you think I'm joking, Katy? I'm aware this is all very stressful for you. But killing you and then having some fun with your parents wouldn't even raise my heart rate. It makes no difference. It's your *choice*. Ring the police. Throw your phone. I'll take whatever you do next as your decision."

Don't you dare throw that phone, Mum snaps in my mind.

But he's clearly serious. If something happens to me, fine. I can live with that. Or maybe not. The panic tightens in my gut. Fine, *fine*, but if this madman hurts my parents… I throw the phone. The car's going too fast for me to hear the phone smash against the concrete, but

I'm sure I heard it anyway. A sound like hope imploding. Whatever that means. My head hurts. Like the situation is clamping it in a vice.

Markus laughs as he closes my window. "You actually did it. Don't they teach you anything in that kung fu school of yours?"

The phrase *kung fu* makes me think of Mum. Just last week she was in the kitchen, practising her 'moves' on Dad, both of them smiling, in love, making me wonder if I'd ever find a man I felt that way about. Or any way.

"That phone was your lifeline. A few words made you abandon it. Jesus Christ. That's just sad."

"A f-f-few words," I whisper. "You threatened to—"

That's as far as I get. He's right. This is just sad: the tears, the uselessness of them. I'm sobbing and shaking like a child. It's so annoying, especially because I've tried to stop several times. Finally, I manage to stop the crying. I wipe angrily at my face.

Cars rush by. We rush by cars. We're just another vehicle going somewhere fast.

"Are you done?" Markus asks.

"Who are you?"

"Markus."

"But who are you to *me*?"

Another chuckle. There's something fake about it. I wonder if he's ever actually laughed in his life. It seems performative. Everything about him does. "Maybe I'm nobody. Or maybe I'm somebody from your deep, dark past."

"I don't have a deep, dark past," I snap. "I was assaulted two years ago. Is that it? Are you a relative of that pathetic freak?"

"Assaulted. You can't even bring yourself to say *it*, can you? What really happened? It was more than an *assault*."

I don't plan to slam my hand against the panel separating us. The impact surges up my arm; it feels surprisingly good. I do it again, again. I keep hitting it, screaming at him. I'm not even sure what I'm saying. Markus doesn't acknowledge my outburst in any way. He just keeps driving.

"Are you done?" he asks when I sit back, drawing in heaving breaths.

"You're a monster."

"Maybe," he says calmly. "I've been called worse. I'm not completely opposed to the idea."

"An animal," I spit. "You're a *worm*."

"Hmm." He shakes his head slowly, as though pondering some intellectual point. "I'd have to disagree with you there. A monster, perhaps… monsters have clear goals. Monsters are bad, but they're intelligent. They want to accomplish something… even if it's just killing the morons in horror flicks. A worm isn't capable of higher thinking: my kind of thinking."

"Oh, so you've got a higher purpose, have you?" I say sarcastically.

"Careful," he says, his tone changing, becoming darker, implying a whole lot of violence. "Don't mock me. Not you, Katy. You can't even talk about what happened to you. It's tragic. How are you supposed to heal if you can't say it? The R-word. The blunt reality of what happened."

My mind rushes back to that night, walking home – the hand, grabbing, dragging me into the dark. And then what came after. The invasion of my body and my soul. The shattering of my resolve as I tried the moves my old martial arts teachers were so proud of. And realising none of them worked. They were all tricks. When I grabbed his arm and tried to twist him around, he just laughed, a backhand across the jaw, knuckles so hard stars exploded in my vision.

Markus drives faster, surging past cars. "Say it." He sounds wild. He pushes down on the pedal, my belly warbling as I fall back against the seat. "Say it, Katy. *Say it.*"

"S-stop." That bloody stutter again, sending me back decades. "Stop it!"

"Tell me what happened to you." We must be going over a hundred now. Far over the speed limit, anyway. I've never felt a car go this fast. "We take motor travel for granted, don't we? Moving at speeds our ancestors would've found inconceivable, with death in our hands. All it would take is a violent turn of my hands. That's all. Then this car would flip over."

"We'd *both* die!" I shout. "You'll kill yourself."

"Pffft. Okay. *Quidquid erit, omnis fortuna ferenda est.* Do you know what that means? It's Virgil."

Something tells me the *all right, love* performance he was putting on when he was simply my so-called taxi driver is over now. "Please slow down."

"I will," he replies calmly. "Once you give me what I want. It's a simple thing. Just state what happened to you. Don't hide it. Don't hide *from* it."

The world is surging by so unbelievably fast now. I'm not normally aware of the speed I'm travelling on the motorway. It's all relative, after all, but now we're like a race car.

"The phrase I used was Latin, by the way." How can he be so *calm* when we're going this fast? I called him an animal, but I feel the primitive response shivering in me, the fight-or-flight dread. He's talking as if we're two friendly strangers passing a lazy Sunday afternoon on a park bench. "It roughly translates to… whatever fortune holds must be accepted. If you accept your fate, life becomes so much easier. I'm ready to die on this road. Are you?"

Vomit slithers up my throat, threatens to choke me. I forcibly swallow it and then push the words out. "I was *raped*, okay? I was raped by a stranger and I've felt useless ever since. *Okay?*"

Finally, he slows the car down. I wait for the sound of sirens. That's what happened after The Incident – is there any point veiling it now? After the assault. The r-r-r… It's difficult to even think. I managed to scream, somebody heard, called the police. The man's in prison now. Is Markus his brother? His cousin?

Markus glances at me in the rear-view with a twisted smile on his face. "Well done. I know that was difficult for you."

"Thanks so much," I say sarcastically.

"You really shouldn't have ditched your phone," Markus says after a moment, sounding like a disappointed parent.

"I didn't have a choice."

"You did," he replies. "You could've delayed, argued. You could've called my bluff… see if I'd actually drive to your parents' house. You could've smashed the window and dragged yourself out of the car—"

"On the motorway? Are you joking?"

"Before, then—"

"I think you're trying to make yourself feel better. If I'm too weak to defend myself, in your eyes, then I deserve whatever's going to happen to me. I deserve to be kidnapped, to be…" I can't finish the sentence. Anything could happen.

"Don't worry," Markus says, which is a frankly insane thing for him to even think in this situation, let alone say. To me. His hostage. "I'm not going to hurt you like that man did." *That man*, he calls him. Maybe he's trying to lead me off the scent. "I have no interest in having sex with a woman who doesn't want to have sex with me. In fact, I find the desire extremely confusing."

Confusing. There's no moral judgement there. He doesn't find it sickening or grotesque, just confusing. He seems to be a cerebral person, thinking through problems, not *feeling* them. I need to find a way to use that to my advantage. But how? Maybe I could try and counsel the psycho.

"You're not going to experience that this evening," he tells me.

"I suppose I should just believe you."

"Believe me or not. It's a fact."

"So what *are* you going to do with me?"

"Whatever I want."

"And what do you want?"

"For you to shut up and stop asking me questions."

I hate how quickly I bite down, silencing myself. It reminds me of the r-r-r… The *Incident*. During that, the attacker – a man called Roger Castle – gave me certain instructions, positions. I had to do what he said. And as I lay there, I promised myself I'd never let myself be so powerless again. That's why I quit my bullshido martial arts and started a proper one.

Would I survive jumping from a car on the motorway? The answer is maybe, but no matter what, I'd be severely injured. If I could look at this situation objectively, I might tell the woman – me – to jump from the car despite the consequences. If something far worse is waiting for me, which seems likely, then the injuries would be worth it. If he's going to kill me – again, likely – then they're *obviously* worth it.

But even if the door wasn't locked, I wouldn't be able to do it. I'll have to wait for my chance. When it comes, I can't hesitate. I can't let myself think. If it comes to violence, I'm no longer under any delusions. I'll probably lose. But I *might* be able to get the upper hand, just for a moment. If that happens, then I'll have to be brutal. Eye gouging is probably my best option.

As we drive – thankfully, at the speed limit – I mentally prepare myself for it. I visualise driving both thumbs into his eyes. I imagine the feeling of his eyeballs, the blood, the voice inside me telling me to stop; this is enough… and then I'll have to keep going. I'll have to kill him.

6

KATY

We take the motorway toward Devon. I press my face against the window, watching the other cars, the countryside whipping past us. With each mile we travel, the desperation in me grows longer teeth, gnaws more fiercely. I'm struggling to imagine a scenario in which I escape unscathed. As well as mentally preparing to inflict vicious damage, I need to ready myself for all the things he could do to me. Sure, he *said* he's not going to repeat The Incident, but trusting him would be a serious mistake on my part.

Finally, he takes an exit, driving into the countryside. The car slows down. Maybe this will give me a chance.

"Do you have any theories about why I'm doing this?" Markus asks conversationally.

"You're a friend of Roger's. The man who…"

His laugh is complex. Judgement for not being able to say it, but also a gruff hint of offence. I've sat across from people for so many hundreds of hours, maybe thousands, I'm able to read them fairly well. But I'm also aware that Markus is probably a psychopath. Not in the colloquial sense, but the strict, medical sort. The kind of person who prides himself on being able to fool normal people like me.

"So you think I was friends with a cracked-out demented freak who'd flashed and molested several women before finally graduating to the main show with you. And, when he was rightfully caught and imprisoned, I waited two years to enact my revenge."

When he lays it all out like that, it makes me feel stupid. But that's exactly what he *would* do if I'd guessed his reason outright at the start. He clearly wants to be in control… and for this to be some kind of game.

"Just because you say it like that," I tell him, "doesn't mean it's not true."

"I can quote Latin. I'm a passable actor, evidenced by the fact you bought my friendly cabby routine—"

"That wasn't your acting," I cut in. "I was waiting for a taxi. A taxi arrived. It had nothing to do with you. In fact, you made me suspicious right away."

His mismatched eyes snap to me in the rear-view. We're driving through a small village, heading toward the countryside. And then… No, I can't let my thoughts go there. If I start speculating about what kind of torture this freak has waiting for me, I won't even be able to speak.

"You bought it," he says. "But if it makes you feel better to pretend you didn't, I understand. You need a small modicum of power. But my point – before you rudely interrupted me – was this. A man like me is not friends with a man like your rapist. Try again."

"I haven't done anything to you. Nothing."

"So you've been a paragon of virtue your entire life?"

"I'm not saying that. I've cheated on boyfriends. Sometimes I go through stages where I drink too much. I've lied. But I've never seriously hurt anybody. I've never done anything that warrants this, Markus. *Nothing*."

"I'm disappointed." He sighs. "I thought, as a counsellor, you'd be more introspective than this. Nobody is perfect."

"I'm not saying I'm perfect. But I don't deserve this."

"Hmm," Markus says. "Maybe, when this is over, I'll tell you why I chose you. I hope you'll understand. That's what you're supposed to do, isn't it? Understand people."

I lean forward. "Help me to understand you, then."

"I thought you were supposed to be the expert."

"I'm not a mind reader."

"And I'm not doing your job for you."

He turns away from the village, driving slowly down a country road. If I could open the door or break the window, now would be the ideal chance to flee. But I also have to think about what *he'll* do if I try to run and fail.

"Where are we going?" I ask.

"Somewhere important. I want to find out who you really are. In our modern, Western world, nobody knows who they are. People have a vague idea. *If X happened, I'd do Z*. But most people, when confronted with an honest assessment of their grit, freeze. They do *nothing*. They haven't conditioned themselves for the reality of violence. Or high-stakes decision-making. Everything is hypothetical. Everything is a comfortable lie we tell ourselves to make reality just a little less terrifying."

"So you're going to test me," I say.

"You could call it that," he replies. "But I prefer to think of it as enlightening you. Showing yourself to yourself. When we reach our destination, you'll have a chance few people get."

"And after? Will you let me go?"

"It depends on what you decide," Markus says.

I don't think he's going to let me go no matter what happens. I need to appeal to his sense of power, his ego. There's nothing self-important pricks like better than believing everybody else sees them as godly as they see themselves. But Markus seems perceptive, meaning I'll have to do it without going too far. I'll have to be subtle about it.

He keeps driving. I watch him, noticing how fluidly he changes gears.

"You're a good driver," I tell him.

Another laugh, this one complex too. It's like he's saying, *That compliment means a lot to me. Even if I know it shouldn't. Even if I know you're only saying it because you think it might save your life*. "Thank you. I was a late bloomer getting my licence."

I almost tell him it doesn't show. But that would be going too far. Instead, I fold my arms and stare out the window. It's too dark for me to see anything. At least there's no light in here, meaning I can't see my reflection. If I saw myself with wide terrified eyes, and panic lacing every feature, I'd lose what little resolve I have left.

My animal instinct seizes me the moment I see where he's taking me. We drive down a bumpy dirt track. His headlights cut across the darkness and rest on a small stone structure. It looks like a farmer's storehouse, maybe, not much bigger than a tollbooth. I almost freak out, hammering at the window, screaming. But what's the point?

Breathe. That's what Joel always tells me during class, especially when I'm grappling with somebody bigger, stronger, and more experienced than me. Everything seems more manageable if a person can breathe slowly and steadily.

But it's tough. Nothing good is going to happen in there. It looks just about big enough for a mattress.

The car comes to a slow stop. Markus turns on the interior light, smiling tightly at me in the rear-view, almost apologetically. "You're going to need to come with me," he says. "It'd be a lot easier if we did this without a fuss."

"What's in there?" I ask, somehow keeping my voice steady.

"A question," he says. "Who are you, Katy?"

"But what is *literally* in there?" I snap. "Enough games. Enough poetry."

"If I told you what was in there, you wouldn't come."

"Do you think *that* makes me want to come?"

"It doesn't matter what you want." He sighs. "With or without a fuss, you're going in there with me."

"If I cause a fuss, as you put it," I say, staring at him directly in the eyes, forcing him to see me as a person… if he's capable of that, "what will you do to me?"

"Whatever's required to get you in there with me," he says. "I've got zip ties, gags, rope. I'm bigger and stronger than you. I know you've been training martial arts, but I highly doubt you're ready for the intensity of violence I'm comfortable employing. I was in a bar fight once and bit a man's nose off. I was quite young. Everybody around me was so shocked. My friend said I must've been terrified to do something like that. I took the hint, told the police yes, I was scared for my life. But the truth was, it was a reasonable assessment; it was the quickest, most efficient way to end the fight. But hey-ho…" He turns this time, instead of looking at me in the rear-view. "What's it going to be, Katy? Either way is fine with me."

If I knew what was going to happen inside that stone structure… would I fight? I *know* it can't be anything good. It's going to be evil. The violence he inflicts on me in there will be so much worse than whatever will happen if I fight. Won't it?

I tell him, "I'll come peacefully."

But inside, I get myself ready. Hurt him – get the car keys – drive away…

7

KATY

I didn't realise how big Markus was, but I do when he climbs from the car. He must be six-three, six-four, with wide shoulders and big burly arms. He leans down and pushes his face against the window, those eerie eyes staring.

"Are you thinking of trying something?" he says, his voice muffled through the glass.

In my mind, I repeat the mantra. *Hurt him – get the car keys – drive away*... "No," I say.

He grins, flashing rows of gleaming white teeth. I can imagine finding him handsome in entirely different circumstances. I stamp on that thought as soon as it arises in my mind. "I don't believe you. You're too tough, Katy. I read the news articles about your assault. You almost tore Roger's left eye out."

"I was panicked," I tell him. "I'm not panicking now."

"No? Tell that to your chest."

I look down, see my chest rising and falling quickly. It's weird. It doesn't *feel* like I'm breathing that fast. It's not like a panic attack. A lot of my clients disassociate. As a counsellor – as opposed to a psychotherapist – it's not my job to diagnose them. But I notice it. The wife dealing with a sandbagging husband, or the woman who feels invisible at work… They'll disconnect, almost *watch* themselves. It's easier than being there. Than being here.

"You can try to run if you want," he says. "Or you can try to fight me. I'll just point out that, so far, I've been extremely civil with you."

"Kidnapping is hardly civil." I regret the retort right away, the moment his lips twitch into a frown. I'm supposed to be winning him over. "But I understand what you mean. You could've been far rougher. You could've hit me or… done other things."

His lips twitch again, this time into a small smile. I'm ashamed by how relieved this makes me feel. "Exactly. That's what I meant. Other men in my position would be doing far worse to you. You're not an unattractive woman, Katy."

My skin slithers. My womb decays and dies in less than a second. The idea of intimacy with this man – honestly, with any man since The Incident – sickens me. But I try not to let him see my reaction. I force a smile to my face. "Thank you so much."

"I'm opening the door now. Don't make me hurt you."

Hurt him – get the car keys – drive away…

As the door slowly opens, I try to will myself into action. It's so easy when watching a film or hearing about a story like this. There's always a point where the inevitable question comes: why didn't she run? Why didn't she fight? Why didn't she *try*?

He opens the door all the way, steps back. Joel often talks about how to determine if somebody can fight back. One indicator is that they will adopt the fighting stance even if they look non-aggressive. Markus does that now, subtly moving one leg behind the other, turning his body, getting ready to strike.

I stand, sucking in the cold night air. The stars are impossibly bright above us without the light pollution of civilisation getting in the way. Markus is close, but not close enough for me to… to what, exactly? Use my two years of white belt experience to incapacitate a man more than twice my size?

"Shall we?" he says, gesturing to the stone structure.

Hurt him – get the car keys – drive away...

I tell myself to leap at him, thumbs straight for the eyes. I'm going to regret doing nothing the moment I'm locked in there with him.

"Shall we?" he repeats, taking a step forward while maintaining his fighting stance.

"Uh, y-yes."

"You're so cute when you stutter," he says, chuckling.

He stands close to my shoulder, not touching, but leaving me in no doubt what would happen if I tried to hurt him. He's so much taller than me. He guides me toward the shack, not pushing me, but by walking briskly, giving me the choice to either move with him or let him move me. Far too quickly, we're at the door. Markus reaches into his pocket.

Now, now. With one hand otherwise occupied, I might be able to…

Just like that, the moment passes. He takes out a key, thrusts it at me. "Open the door."

"What are you going to do to me?"

"I've already told you. I'm going to test you."

"If you're going to…"

"Jesus *Christ*." He runs a hand through his hair. "You can say it. *Rape*. It won't hurt you. Reality is reality. All the euphemisms in the world won't change that."

He looms over me, staring. He's neither smiling nor frowning now. Instead, his expression is one of complete calm. Almost like he's hollowed himself out. He's ready to do whatever it takes to force me to follow his orders. With no choice – that's a lie; I could drive the key into his eye, turn and run, something, anything – I slip the key into the lock. It feels impossibly cold against my hand.

When I see it, I gasp, drop the key. Markus laughs. There's nothing complex about this one. It's pure joy. I almost scream when he claps me on the shoulder, as if we're friends, as if we're about to do something wholesome and productive together.

8

HIM

The internet is an interesting and often terrifying place. I don't mean to say that *I'm* terrified, but regular people should be. If one knows the right places to look, anything can be found. The most grotesque and unique forms of torture – inflicted upon every kind of person imaginable – drugs, weapons, lonely echoing caves of politics and religion. It's all there, all the time, allowing a person to consume more information in an hour than our ancestors would've their entire lives.

It was simple to find Patrick. I made an account on a Dark Web deviant website. The images on that forum were shocking, even to me. I remember when I was a kid, the prayers my mother would say after she handled her business. She'd kneel and gesture and mutter about God and Satan. The stuff on this forum was a product of Satan. It had to be.

Patrick was an active member of these forums. He would comment on the photos and videos the other members submitted as though leaving an online review. One sticks in my head. *I wish she would've smiled more.* I'm often torn between branding myself entirely emotionless – as people have before – and accepting I have some degree of humanity. The girl Patrick was talking about could not have possibly smiled. If I had somehow slithered into the video, put a gun to her head and asked if I should pull the trigger, she would've begged me to do it. Yet Patrick's only concern was that she should've *seemed* happier.

Making contact wasn't difficult, though it did involve some unsavoury role-playing. I had to pretend to be as debased as the other members of the forum. Just like in all realms of life, there was a hierarchy. The method of rising within this one involved condoning, encouraging, and celebrating the actions of the video and photo posters. This meant stating things in the exact opposite way to how I perceived them. A horror became a delight. A sin became a virtue.

Finally, I'd earned Patrick's trust. He private messaged me, asking if *I'd* like to upload some videos or photos. Instead, I offered him one better: a live experience. That's what I called it. Defusing the true nature of it via language. People do that all the time. *We need to have a talk* easily becomes *I'm going to leave you and utterly obliterate the foundation upon which you've built your life: your character*. Patrick took some convincing. He was rightfully suspicious.

If I seem like I somewhat despise regular people, it's because I do. There are countless Patricks in the world. They are standing behind you in the supermarket and making small talk with you at the charity shop; they offer you a small smile on the bus and go out of their way to help you with your garden work. But if confronted with that fact, most regular people will wilfully close their eyes.

Regular people will allow one thousand children to be abused in the most twisted ways as long as they don't have to look, fully and honestly, at *one* child. Out of sight, out of mind. It wasn't always this way. Read history; people used to be tough. But not us. We let the bad guys do any damn thing they want as long as we don't have to *hear* about it. It's pathetic.

I remember, once, I was at a barbeque talking with a single mother of two. I'd recently watched a popular film about child trafficking, and mentioned this to her. Her response? She covered her ears, actually *closed her eyes* – I wish I was making this up – and told me, "I can't hear that." If I'd given into my natural response, I would've grabbed her by the hair and pressed her face into the dirt. Then I would've told her, *"Maybe you don't want to hear it, but there are people out there who want to kidnap and hurt your children. If you're not willing to at least acknowledge that, how will you ever stop it?"*

Most *regular* people are woefully unprepared for what life truly is. Even Patrick, who by his very nature should've been ready for a violent altercation, crumpled the moment he took a stiff right hand to the nose. I'll always remember him sitting on the floor with both hands clasped to his leaking nose, staring up at me with wide and stupid eyes, this man who'd encouraged and participated in the worst acts a person can do…

He was so *shocked.* People always are. It pisses me off, honestly. It really annoys me. Shock is a modern luxury. We're so soft. We're so presumptuous. We always think somebody else will be there. A spouse, a friend, the government. Somebody will save us.

But not Patrick. And not Katy. Nobody is saving them. Nobody is saving me.

9

KATY

There's a lamp in the corner of the room, throwing harsh light onto the skeletal figure hunched in the corner. He's an elderly man, a thin beard sprouting from sunken cheeks. His eyes are pits of pure terror. His legs are tied together with thick rope, his hands secured in front of him with zip ties. The room reeks of human waste. He's sitting in a pool of it. His clothes are threadbare and stained. There's something about his reaction that tells me he's been here for a few days at least. He stares as if to say, *What now?*

"Hello, Patrick," Markus says from behind me.

"Puh-please," Patrick whispers.

My blood turns cold. I've read that phrase so many times. I've always thought it was a cliché. But my blood is ice.

"Please," Markus repeats. "I don't understand how you can use that word after what you've done. *They* said please, didn't they…"

Patrick looks at me. "Puh-puh-please."

"They know how to seem like victims," Markus says. "The predators of the world. Isn't that right, Patrick? You've perfected that particular art?"

I'm trapped between the old man on the floor and Markus standing directly behind me. I almost puke again when a waft of nauseating filth hits me in the face, up my nose, tickling the back of my throat.

"I asked you a question." Markus walks into the tiny, cramped room and closes the door. There's barely enough space for me to press myself against the wall. "Well?"

"Yes," Patrick whispers. "But that was a different life."

"Pfft. A different life. Tell my friend here what you do."

"I don't—"

"Tell my friend what you do or I'll peel your fingernails off one by one."

Patrick shudders, looking so pitiful, looking so broken, like he needs help. "I do bad things to children…"

My body gets even colder. I flinch when Markus snaps, "No euphemisms. No veiled language. Tell her *precisely* what you do."

Patrick swallows. For a second, I think he's going to argue. But then he lowers his gaze and says, "I molest and rape children. I'm also an admin on a Dark Web forum where we share photos and videos."

"Bingo," Markus says. "That wasn't so difficult, was it?"

"Plea—"

"If you say *please* one more fucking time, I swear to God, I'll beat you to death. Be quiet." Markus squeezes by me. Did he lock the door? Did he pick up the key after I dropped it? There's nothing between me and the only exit now. Hairs prick on the back of my neck. A strange tingle moves over my body. Markus kneels, resting his forearms on his knees. He's at a sideways angle, but it's still the most vulnerable he's been since I climbed into his taxi. "Why do you think you're here, Patrick?"

Patrick leans as far from Markus as he can get. It's so messed up. Even knowing what this man has done, I feel pity for him. But wait – *has* he done those things? Maybe Markus has kidnapped an innocent man and forced him to make these claims. "To repent for my sins," Patrick says.

"Pfft. No, my friend. The time for that is long, long, long past. I don't care what your religion says. Or the sick fucks you talk to online. There's no repentance for people like you. Once you cross that line, even in thought, you're rabid. Nothing to do but put you down."

Markus stands, rolls his shoulders. "That's why you're here, Katy. You've spent your life helping people who've suffered in the most depraved ways… you might have even counselled some of Patrick's victims. He's an old man; he's been doing this for a long while."

"I don't understand," I say.

"I think you do," he replies, with a mocking smile. "You spend your days helping people overcome their trauma. It's an admirable profession. But how serious are you about your work, Katy? Are you willing to *prevent* trauma?"

I shake my head. He's right. I know what he's asking me. But, despite practising violence on a semi-regular basis, the idea of brutally killing an elderly man… He's evil, though. Isn't he? And what if Markus makes me choose – Patrick or myself?

"Words, Katy," Markus snaps.

"I haven't got any evidence he's done what you say he's done."

"What *I* say he's done?" Markus tuts. "That's not a fair assessment of the situation. *He* said it. Not me."

"But you could've made him."

"Oh, Jesus Christ." Markus massages the bridge of his nose, closes his eyes for a moment. It's another chance for me to do something. A sudden strike – turn – push the door open. Wait, did he push it inward or does it open outward? What if I waste time trying to push a pull door and… And my chance is gone. He's staring at me again. "So you think I kidnapped a random, innocent old man and brought him here so I could watch you pointlessly murder him. This isn't *random*. This has *meaning*."

"There's no way for me to know."

"You're being a coward," he says.

"Because I don't want to kill somebody I know absolutely nothing about? And, for the record, trying to make me feel stupid for questioning you is, itself, stupid."

A thin smile. He nods slowly. "Fair enough. So what you're saying is, if you had evidence, you'd do the right thing. You'd kill this worm."

Patrick shudders from his place on the floor, but he doesn't say anything.

Fear tries to make my voice small. I push past it. Try to, anyway. "If I d-did that, would you let me go?"

"I d doubt it," he says, mocking my stutter with easily readable glee. "But it might stop me from doing some rather nasty things to you."

"I don't like the word *might*."

"Enough games," Markus says, reaching into his pocket.

I back up against the door. His hand squirms in his pocket like an animal searching for a throat to bite. Looking for the kill. "Relax," he says, taking out his phone. "One of us didn't stupidly throw ours onto the motorway. I want to show you something."

There's that feeling again, the chill in my veins. "I don't want to see it."

"You have to. I'm sorry. If you try to stop me, I'll force you to watch it."

"I can't look at s-s-s…" Fucking *stutter*. "Something like that."

"That makes no sense. How can you hide from the grimy side of life when your job is built on it?"

"My job is to help peop—"

"You'll help people on a far greater level, with a far greater reach, if you end this sap. Right. Here we go." He presses a few buttons on his phone and then turns it to me.

I avert my gaze. I know what it's going to be. *Evidence*. I can't have images like that branded on my mind. I've *heard* about this sort of thing, of course, often in painful detail. But I've never seen it. I've never needed to. My imagination is vivid enough.

"Katy," he says firmly. "Last chance to watch it willingly."

"You can't make me," I whisper.

"But I can. It would be a simple case of inflicting enough pain. You wouldn't want to fight then. Either way, you're going to watch this video. You have to make an intelligent judgement here."

If I'm going to get out of this, I can't be injured. My chances while unharmed are low enough as it is. "F-fine."

He nods. "That's the correct decision. Please put your hands behind your back."

"Why?"

"I don't want you to try to steal my phone. It wouldn't be good for you."

Slowly, I do what he says, clasping my hands together. I'm sweaty all over. I can feel a hot line of sweat sliding down my side. Markus turns the phone and taps the screen. The video shows a dark bedroom with a child sitting on top of the covers, their knees drawn to their chest. The door opens. It's Patrick, very clearly the same old man who's sitting on the floor.

He walks toward the child and…

"Don't look away," Markus says.

"I get the point."

"You have to watch."

"I've seen en—"

Markus moves far faster than I would've guessed for a man his size. He darts his hand out and grabs my face, not roughly, exactly, but not soft either. He turns my face so I'm staring at the screen.

I won't tell you what I see. There's no need. I won't tell you what I hear coming from his phone. You know what it is. You know what's happening. You know what Patrick did.

"Go on," Markus says, once the video is over. "Tell me it's not real. Tell me it's a deep fake. Keep running."

"I'm going to be sick," I say, covering my mouth.

"Are you trying to trick me, Katy?"

"I..." Before I can finish, I keel over, a hot stream of vomit slithering up my throat and bursting from my lips.

"I guess not," he says. "Look what she's done to your room, Pat. That's not very good, is it?"

"I'm sorry," the old man whispers. "I'm so sorry."

"Oh, shut up. She's seen what you are. She's not going to pity you now."

I stand, wiping my mouth. My eyes are watery. It brings back memories of university, mornings after nights out, my friends joking I always looked like I was crying when I was hungover. They'd bring me tissues and pat me on the back... or jokingly bring me shots of whisky or vodka as *medicine*. That world seems so distant from this one.

"You're going to make this right," Markus says, reaching into his inside jacket pocket. He takes out a Stanley knife and pushes the blade up. Then – is he serious? – he *hands me the knife*. The metal handle is cold against my hand, driving home the reality. I'm holding a weapon. Markus is unarmed.

10

HIM

People unaccustomed to violence and stress – real stress, not the humdrum panic everyday life instils – are terrible at masking their intentions. I watch Katy's features twitch in excitement and anticipation, and then she purposefully flattens her lips. She narrows her eyes. She's thinking about killing me, obviously. It's not a huge leap. I'm her kidnapper and I've just given her a weapon. But she's also wondering why I'd be so confident doing something like that. The truthful answer is that I'd like it if she tried. It would be interesting, at the very least.

She licks her lips, probably because they're bone-dry. Her hair was already scraggly from her workout, and now it's like seaweed. "But what do I get?" she asks. Her cheeks pale with the effort of forcing this question out. This is all so surreal for her.

"It's what you *don't* get," I tell her. "No broken bones. No black eyes. No casket. It's a good deal."

"So if I don't do this, you're going to hurt me?"

"Stop asking stupid questions."

She stands up straighter. All the while, Patrick is still on the floor, trussed-up and powerless, exactly like his victims were. He whimpers continuously. I can't even imagine how he can be this self-pitying after what he's done. Of course, I'd never do something like that. If I somehow shared his particular brand of twisted desire, I'd do the right thing and take my own life.

Finally, Katy speaks, "I don't think you're going to do that. You're not a bad person."

"Maybe not," I allow. "That doesn't mean I'm a good one."

"No – fine. I get that. But you're a reasonable person. You clearly have a plan for this evening. Something tells me it doesn't involve you beating me into a bloody pulp. How would I participate in your... *experience* then?"

I'm proud of her. She's got her stutter under control. And she was right to choose the word *experience* carefully. That's precisely what it is. I can't help but smirk. She's right... for now. I don't want to hurt her yet. I haven't decided what I'm going to do with her when this is over.

"Don't you want to kill him?" I ask.

"I don't want to kill anyone."

"But..." I take a moment to choose my next words. This would be a gift for many people. The chance to take out a pervert, a monster, with no repercussions. "You saw the video. Surely you agree the world is better without him."

"Yes."

"But you can't do it."

She flinches. "N-not under these circumstances."

"No, no, no," I say. "That's a lie. You'd never be able to do it. You're a goddamn coward. You'd rather wait for him to abuse more children so they can grow up and then send you an email. *I'm working through some trauma, please overcharge me for hours and hours and hours so I can come to the obvious conclusion I should just let it go.*"

I don't realise what's happening until I've got her pressed right up against the wall. I'm not proud of losing control. It happens sometimes. It's like a miniature blackout. Katy is shivering, the knife raised, complete animalistic terror captivating every single one of her features. All her martial arts training has fluttered out of her head when confronted with a demon: the spectre of real violence. She can't even hold the knife steady.

Insanely, I almost apologise. Instead, I take a step back, raise my hands, try to smirk. But there's still the beast in me. The devil. "I suppose I should submit myself to God," I say, thinking of my father, my mother, my life, my pain. Fuck me. I'm being so self-pitying. "Then good ol' Satan will submit before me, right?"

"Puh-puh-puh…"

Katy's trying to say *please*, but she can't even force the word out.

"I know," I tell her. "It's not how you imagined it."

She leans against the wall. It's like I can see the events of the evening catching up with her, spirits slithering into this small farmer's storehouse, slipping into her body. The farmer thinks I'm using this to store drugs. He was happy to take the payment and turn a blind eye. I could kill them both, or kill us all, and he'd only find out days or weeks later, whenever he bothered to check.

"Let's make a deal," I tell her. "I'll up the stakes. Gut Patrick. Take this mongrel's life. And I swear, Katy…" I hold my hand up. "I swear to God. I swear on my life, I'll let you go."

Patrick whimpers from the floor. I snap again. Not a blackout this time. I wilfully spin and lean into a swift, low left hook. He tries to duck out of the way. But he doesn't do so well against grown-ups. He cries out like a coward when my knuckle drives into his chin and sends him sprawling, awkward because of the zip ties.

When I turn back, I see Katy has taken a step forward closer to Patrick, the knife aimed as if she's trying to will herself to do it.

"I can't trust you."

I groan. "Stop this now. I've set my terms. I'm telling the

truth. You don't *want* to trust me because you don't want to kill this man, which is, frankly, confusing to me."

"The video's real?" she says.

"We're going in circles. Kill him and I'll give you my phone, leave the car and the keys, and walk into the countryside."

I didn't plan on this part. There's more to come yet. But I mean it. I'm telling the truth. If she manages to overcome her instinctive empathy and butcher this monster like he deserves, tonight will have been a success.

"I didn't do it," Patrick whispers when Katy kneels in front of him.

"She saw the video, Patrick. Take this with some dignity."

"How many?" Katy says, her voice hoarse. She's trying to work up to it. When Patrick doesn't reply, she moves the knife toward him. There's no deadly intent behind the movement, but it's a start. Even better when she raises her voice. "*How many*?"

"How many what?" Patrick says.

"You know what she's asking." I stand behind Katy, looking down at the pervert. If Katy had the grit, she could turn and drive the blade into my leg, maybe give herself enough time to escape.

"I don't know," Patrick whispers.

"Why don't you know?" I ask.

Patrick blinks, realises his mistake. His eyes are watering.

"You lost count," Katy says, a stunned sort of awe in her voice.

Patrick moans and looks away. Looks *away*. It's unacceptable. I could never respect somebody who's done what he has, but if he did it, then faced his fate… if he owned it… no, I still wouldn't respect him. But I'd despise him just a little less.

"Go on, Katy. It's simple. He can't fight. Don't think about it. Just drive the blade under his ear, then drag it across. There will be some resistance, but you can do it. I'll hold his head in place if you like."

She glances up at me, blinks. "C-could you?"

I walk behind Patrick. It's difficult because of the space. Kneeling, I grab the back of his head, tilt it to expose his throat. Katy's thinking about hurting me again. That's okay. Unless she's incredibly lucky with her lunge, she's unlikely to kill me. I keep my palms facing down, my chin slightly tucked, and use Patrick's body to block mine.

"And you'll let me go," Katy says.

"Circles, circles. Get on with it."

Now, she switches between thinking about hurting me to genuinely trying to psyche herself up to hurting Patrick. She grits her teeth. Pushes the blade against his ear. Predictably, Patrick is whining and moaning and playing the victim. Seconds pass, thirty, then a minute.

Katy yells and falls back, sitting heavily. "I c-can't."

I sigh. "Understandable. Give me the knife, then. I'm going to have to tie you up and gag you."

"Then what are you going to do?" she asks, delivering each word deliberately, probably in an effort to stop the stutter.

"I'm going to cut and stab Patrick until he dies."

"Please, I didn't—"

Patrick groans when I slide the blade up, dart my hand out, and give him a quick jabbing shank in the ribs. I feel the blade scrape against his bone. He whines and falls onto his side. I stab him again, feeling the warmth of the blood.

Oh, Christ. Katy's having some kind of meltdown. She's breathing hard and shaking all over. She bangs her head against the wall.

"Careful," I tell her, not wanting her to ruin the evening. "Katy…"

"Duh-duh-don't m-m-make…"

"I get it." Standing, I tuck the knife into my pocket. "Just calm down. It's only a bit of blood. Can't you even *watch* me do it?"

"Let me out." She crawls toward the door. "Please, Markus. Let me out."

I should make her watch, really. It would do her some good. But she seems to be on the verge of becoming completely useless. Giving Patrick a remindful kick in the leg, I say, "Wait here, all right, chum?"

He moans, blood soaking his tatty clothes, making the room reek of harsh metal. It's repulsive.

11

KATY

"Breathe, stay calm." I hear Joel in my mind, the black-belt instructor who never loses his cool and is capable of rolling out of any situation. "*That's always the main thing, Katy. Just breathe.*"

But I can't breathe. I barely feel *here* when Markus hooks one hand under my armpit and hauls me to my feet. He leads me outside with far more kindness than I would've expected. I think – hope – his broken bones threat was just that. A threat. He leads me to the car.

"I'm going to have to tie you up," he says. "You understand."

It's not a question. Shamefully, I'm in no state to fight. When I saw Markus casually drive the knife into Patrick's frail ribs, it was like The Incident all over again, the fracturing, the disconnect. All my plans of somehow using the blade on Markus disappeared into a pit of uselessness inside of me. I can't even answer Markus as he starts trussing me up Christmas-turkey-style. That's what I am, as useless as dead meat. I need to get a *grip*.

He pushes me face-first into the backseat and zip ties my

hands in front of me. After that, he places a hand on my shoulder from behind and pushes me down into an excruciating, unnatural position.

"This isn't going to be comfortable," he says, zip-tying my wrists to my ankles. The dull ache in my lower back seems distant. It's funny; my back has been giving me issues for weeks. But this is the first time I've felt it since getting into this taxi. "Right…" Markus takes a step back, rubbing his hands together. I'm not sure if he realises he's smearing blood on himself. "Let me handle this. Then we're off."

"O-o-o…" *Off where?*

"You'll be okay," he says, slamming the door before walking toward the stone structure. At least, that's what I assume he's doing.

It would be so easy to devolve into panic. But I have to focus. Just breathe. That's step one. If I can breathe, I can think… about what *I* want. Not the knife disappearing into the dirty shirt, the stench of metal, blood, the petal blooming… not the knife slipping in like the monster who assaulted me slipped…

And now I'm slipping, my thoughts cascading. Fucking *breathe*, Katy. Slowly in, slowly out, I let each one come and go. I'm getting impatient with myself. Ideally, I'd spring into action right now. But I have to be somewhat calm first. This gets more difficult when I hear it, him, the screams, the sounds of what Markus is doing to Patrick.

He deserves it, I tell myself as Patrick wails. The sound is muffled because of the stone walls and the car windows, but it's still there. Breathe, breathe… Finally, my head begins to clear. My throat hurts from the contorted position I was in. There isn't much time to think.

Job one: zip ties. I can't waste any time looking for a knife. Brazilian jujitsu has massively helped my flexibility. I bring my feet up, hunching my body even more, allowing me to bite down on the ties around my feet. The angle is painful, but I ignore it, ignore everything, the screams, the doubt. Biting down, I begin to gnaw back and forth. As long as the murderous noises are still happening, Markus is still busy.

I use my teeth like a saw, over and over. But it doesn't do anything. My teeth aren't sharp enough. More panic – get *lost*. Instead of gnawing, I bite down and then pull backward, forcing my feet down at the same time, as if I'm trying to break the grip of somebody holding on to me.

It hurts, badly. My teeth feel like they're going to pop out of my mouth before the tie breaks. It doesn't matter, though. If I have to leave here toothless, at least I'll be alive. At least I won't have to listen to the… No, the screams have stopped. The next try, I pull so hard it's a miracle I don't seriously injure myself. Or maybe I have and I'm just too amped-up to realise.

Snap. The tie breaks. My mouth pulses in agony. With my feet free, I get to work on the ties securing my hands. But what if Markus returns? There's no more noise. Everything is horribly quiet. My breathing and my panic deafen me to everything else.

Leaning up, I look out the front of the car. The shed door is opening, showing a flash of light… showing a glimpse of the walls. There's red everywhere. Slick and glistening. When Markus appears, I quickly lower my head, pretending I'm still tied up. I've had far too many chances so far. He gave me a weapon and I froze like an idiot. But not this time. I'm going to do something. I can't wait to find out what warped plan he has next.

Breathe, breathe, breathe…

I hear him just outside the car. When he knocks on the window – three quick fingernail taps – I flinch. Look up. He's smiling at me, almost sadly, blood smeared across his face, blood in his hair. There's even blood on the window from where he tapped against it.

"I did what you couldn't," he says. "Silly, silly Katy. Did you hear how easy that was? I barely had to use the knife." He hits the window, harder this time. "I said, did you *hear*?"

"Yes. I heard." I make sure to keep my head low, looking at him out of the corner of my eye.

"And – your verdict? Was it the right thing?"

"Yes."

"You're not just saying that, are you?"

"No."

He nods. "Good. Now come and see what I did. You have to look at this, at least. This is true violence. This is what happens when you strip away the wallpaper of society. Come on…"

He opens the door. This is it. One of many chances I've had. That internal block tries to rise up again, tries to stop me from doing what I know I have to. But I can't listen to that voice.

The second he opens the door, I spring at him. "*If you're going to act, act. Don't hesitate*." That was Joel again, talking about real-world scenarios. I launch at Markus like a torpedo, driving my tied hands at his face as hard as I can, pushing with my legs to generate force. He roars when my knuckle catches him in the nose. A *crunch*, and then he stumbles backwards, just a couple of steps.

I slither out the car, turn, duck my head, run. I don't try to hit him again. He's already recovering. I spring past Patrick's tomb – catching a quick surreal glimpse of his swollen face, one eye staring almost like an accusation – and then into the field beyond it. Pumping my legs, I try to remember to breathe. But I'm choking with the panic. How close is he? Is he chasing me? Where *is* he?

The grass is mulchy beneath my feet, trying to swallow my

footsteps. It's difficult to keep balance with my hands tied, like one giant fist swinging back and forth with each stride. Behind me, I hear *squelch-squelch-squelch*, quicker than I'm moving. I have to be faster. I can't let him catch up. If he does…

No, I can't think that. Just keep moving.

12

HIM

I almost laugh, but that would waste valuable energy. I need all the air I can get too, since she's busted my nose up quite badly. It doesn't feel broken, but the pain is inconvenient. Plus, my body is a little sore from what I did to Patrick; admittedly, I got carried away. Katy is putting in a good effort, her silhouette twenty or so feet ahead of me, her body swinging side to side in an exaggerated manner, most likely because her hands are still tied.

But still, the urge is there, to let out a long, proud laugh. She finally did something. All right, so she didn't do what I wanted. It would've been far better for us both, and for her future life, if she'd killed the lowlife. But this is the next best thing. She's not a trapped rat anymore; she's graduated to a scurrying rodent.

She's getting us both filthy though. This field feels like it's sitting atop standing water. Each step threatens to send me plummeting down. I jog after her carefully, breathing slow, letting the murderous adrenaline drain out of me. The field stinks worse than the killing did. Shit and mud and damp.

I'm perhaps ten feet away now. She's reached a border of

trees and large bushes, running up one side of it. There's no way she's going to find a way through before I get to her.

Five feet… She must hear me. She spins, putting her back against a tree, far too exhausted from the little jaunt she's just led me on. But it's not just the physical exertion, of course. She raises her joined hands, looking around frantically, as if for a weapon.

I left the knife with Patrick. Maybe that was a mistake.

"What now?" I ask her casually.

"We can end this here," she says, with admirable control of her stutter again, especially considering the circumstances. "Just turn around. Walk away. Get in the car. I never saw you, okay, Markus? I'll say a man kidnapped me. I didn't see his face. He brought me here and then I managed to get away. That's it. Nobody has to know about this."

I take a small step forward, watching her reaction. She's getting ready for a fight. Finally. "You don't get to decide that."

Suddenly, she kneels, picks up a large rock. I raise my hands, ready for her to throw it. I've also put my feet in a fighting stance, one behind me and one forward, body slightly angled, giving her a smaller target.

"J-just leave me alone!"

"Oh, okay," I say sarcastically. "You've convinced me."

She throws her head back and screams, *"Help! Help! Help!"*

It's unlikely anybody is out here at this time of night – it's gone ten – but there's a chance. So I need to shut her up. I lurch forward suddenly. She reacts: a clumsy throw of the rock. I'm able to sidestep and then run right at her. She's got good instincts. She takes a fighting stance too, tries to hammer my face. I slip to the other side and then deliver a seventy per cent shot to her body. I don't completely turn into it, but I let her feel the power.

She croaks, keeling over… No, ah, *clever*. She pretended to keel over and now she's trying to take me down, using her Brazilian jujitsu skills. But it's a clumsy effort. Her head is way too high, allowing me to quickly slide my arm around her neck and drive my forearm up into her throat. I push with my hips, almost lifting her off the ground.

She gasps and – okay, *now* I laugh – she starts tapping my hip like this is a training session.

"This is the real world now, Katy," I tell her, as her legs flap uselessly. "It's time for you to go to sleep."

She keeps fighting. It takes around eight to ten seconds for the average person to become unconscious from a well-applied guillotine choke. She's out in seven, her legs becoming limp. Slowly, I lower her to the ground, being careful not to drop her. I *should* hurt her, honestly, but I've always found it difficult to hit women. Choking them is easier because I don't have to feel the impact of their frail bodies against my knuckles or forehead or knees or elbows or shins.

Once she's down, I lift her into a fireman's hold. She wakes when we're about halfway back to the car.

"Don't," I snap, when she starts struggling again. "That was a good effort, Katy. My nose is in a lot of pain."

"You could've killed me."

"True. You tapped as if I was going to let go. It was pretty funny. I doubt you see the humour in it, though."

"Size matters," she mutters, more to herself than to me. Holding her like this feels vaguely intimate. I can feel her neck moving when she speaks.

"I've got skill too," I tell her. "I boxed for fifteen years. And I've trained MMA for five. But yes, even without that experience, I think I could've handled you."

"Because you're a man?" She sounds tired and distant, as though she isn't fully conscious yet. It's not just the fact I choked her out, of course. It's also the circumstances: everything she's seen, heard, smelled. It's understandable she'd want to disconnect. But that's a coward's way out.

I leave the mulchy field and walk across the dirt road toward the car. "I'm bigger and stronger than you. I'm far more accustomed to violence. And yes, I have an advantage as a man. I know that's probably very shocking for a modern lady to hear." When she says nothing, I go on, "I have thicker bones. The quality of my muscles is different. My reflexes are faster. Men were put here to keep women safe through violence. Women were put here to keep men in check. It worked extremely well for thousands of years until this oh-so progressive era we currently find ourselves in."

"A political debate," Katy mutters. "You're trying to draw me into a debate *now*."

I carry her to the backseat of the taxi, lower her down, always cautious she's going to try something. Once inside the taxi, she glares up at me. Both of us are covered in filth. We stink of mud and shit.

Reaching up, I softly touch my nose. It's stopped bleeding, at least, but something feels out of place. The cartilage is shifting around. I'll need to get it looked at, but I can tolerate the pain and the disrupted breathing for tonight. "I'm going to give you a choice of punishments," I say. "Either I cut off your pinkie finger… or you clean up Patrick's mess for me. Your choice. You have five seconds to decide."

She must be getting the point now; she doesn't take the full five seconds. "I'll clean up," she says quickly.

"All right. But try anything again…"

She blinks. Tears in her eyes. Maybe she wants pity. "Are you going to kill me tonight?"

I almost reply, *I'm saving you. I'm making you look at reality, honestly and bluntly*. But she deserves to suffer after that display. She deserves to believe it could all end here.

13

KATY

"Do you tell your clients to face something if it scares them?" Markus says from the doorway. "Or do you tell them to avoid it?"

He's speaking so casually. It's like we didn't just have a mad dash through the dark. My body feels sore all over. My throat hurts from the choke, and my head still feels light. In the two years I've trained jujitsu, I've never passed out. I've always tapped – and had the tap respected. But there's no tapping in reality. I'm only alive right now because, for whatever reason, Markus wants it that way. Which means he has something else planned.

"Katy?" he growls. "This doesn't work if you stand there with your eyes closed. You look like an idiot."

He's right. I've pushed myself against the wall and shut my eyes tightly.

"Are you going to make me peel your eyes open?"

Before he can approach, I forcibly open my eyes, stare down at the mess. He wants me to be here, to fully experience the massacre, but I can't. I have to retreat deep inside myself. I have to pretend this isn't happening. He's right; I advise my clients, for the most part, to intelligently and measuredly face their fears. But this is… it's not fear. It's something more primal.

Patrick is not human. He was inhuman before his death. That *video…* But Markus has turned him into blood and meat and bone and not much else. The walls are caked with spatters of red. His body is twisted up. The room reeks so badly I almost vomit again. I think the only reason I don't is because my throat hurts too much just thinking about it.

"What do I have to do?" I whisper.

"Job one: get him outside."

I approach the body… then keel over. There's nothing left in me to puke up, but my body contorts anyway, belly tightening. I dry heave, almost fall. But if I did, it would basically mean landing on top of the corpse. Markus sighs impatiently from behind me. I remember his threat… cutting my finger off. I have to do this.

Once the heaves have passed, I grab Patrick around the ankles, telling myself I'm helping a friend move. That's all. This is a martial arts training dummy, stunningly realistic, but it was never a person. Nothing violent or monstrous happened in this tiny space. Just a training dummy.

My muscles protest as I drag him toward the door.

"Okay, that's enough," Markus says.

I drop Patrick's ankles, turn, expecting to see Markus holding a weapon. I haven't performed well enough. I'm a dancing monkey but my moves are too slow. But he's leaning against the door frame, dabbing at his nose with a wet wipe, smirking like a dickhead.

"I'm going to burn this place," he says. "I just wanted to see if you'd do it. Let's get you in the car. This time, I'm going to have to tie you up with rope and put you in the boot." When I open my mouth to argue, he snaps, "That's your fault, not mine. You can sit in the car when we're on the road. But for now… unless you're going to fight me?"

He pushes away from the door, standing to his full height. He looks *bored* by the idea of me fighting him. There's no point. I have to go back to my original plan. Try to win him over psychologically.

"That would be a mistake," I say.

"Obviously," he replies. "Let's go, then. It'll give you some time to think about how you want the rest of this evening to go."

"Where are we going next? You said we'd be on the road."

Markus taps his nose. "Nah-uh. That's not how this works."

In the boot, in total darkness, I let my mind wander back over my life. After The Incident, everybody told me not to blame myself. I was walking home alone, through a quiet park. I had every right to do that, people said, and I agreed. I tried not to blame myself. But now, I have to search for a reason. There must be *some* blame to be had.

I shift to relieve some of the pressure in my shoulder. The ropes dig into me as I think about my counselling clients. I have a large number of women seeking relationship and career advice, a few current and recovering addicts, and one or two men mostly dealing with childhood issues. But I can't think of anything I would've said during these meetings to warrant this.

Maybe Markus is the boyfriend of one of the women I counselled. Maybe he thinks I advised them to break up with him? That's possible, though I've never actually given that advice. As a counsellor, I try not to give *any* advice. My job is to help the client come to their own conclusions. But it doesn't mean Markus sees it that way. He is clearly anti-feminist, judging by the way he was speaking.

Or maybe it has something to do with when I was a kid? I was mostly a good person during my childhood. But there was one summer when, feeling so ashamed about my stutter, I joined in with the bullying of one of the neighbourhood boys. Stinky Steve, we imaginatively called him, once chasing him up a tree and making him stay there for several hours, hurling names up at him. For pathetic, embarrassing, cruel hours, I was so relieved not to be the victim, I didn't care about the pain we caused. But I was the one who eventually ended it. I lost friends because I turned tattletale, and I didn't regret it. I hate that I was ever involved in that. Would Stinky Steve, or one of his friends, really blame me? And anyway, that was *years* ago.

Only a few moments after driving away, we pull over. My belly swims with anxiety. The boot opens and Markus glares down at me. "Have I made my point?"

I'm ashamed at how small my voice is. "Yuh-yes."

He leans down and grabs my arm. "Good. You weren't supposed to spend this night in darkness. In fact, it's all about the light."

14

KATY

"Bloody stinks in here," Markus grumbles as we pull away from the burning structure, the flames bursting from the doorway. "Thanks for that. Now we get to drive for hours reeking of mud and shit and a farmer's field."

I lean against the seat to relieve some of the tension in my body. As we pull away, I watch the flames in the rear-view. It looks like a film… no, that's the last time I think something like that. Hard to believe or not, from now on, I accept that this is happening. I'm no use if I keep obsessing about how surreal this feels.

"Aren't you worried about somebody finding this?" I ask.

"Oh, they will," Markus replies. "They'll identify the body. They might even discover that Patrick was exchanging emails with me – well, the identity I created to trap the freak. But no, I'm not worried. Whatever's going to happen will happen. It won't interfere with tonight."

"You're not scared of going to prison?"

"Pftt. Scared."

"Oh, so you're not scared of anything?"

Despite his busted nose – it looks slightly out of place – and the mud streaking his clothes, he's back to his smirking routine. "I'm capable of assessing situations and realising when I'm at risk. But I'm not afraid. It's useless. It doesn't help people."

The flames get smaller and smaller in the rear-view, until we turn a corner and they're gone entirely. Surely people will see the smoke… but it's so remote, so dark. It might be days before anybody finds Patrick. And even if they did, that doesn't automatically mean they'll be able to find *us*. I'm on my own tonight.

"Fear can fuel some people," I reply. "It can motivate them. I wouldn't have tried to run if I wasn't scared."

"Maybe. But if you'd been able to keep your cool, stay completely calm, *while* running, you would've done far, far better. You might have even got away. You would've made sure to incapacitate me after your sucker punch. Then you could've taken the keys."

I stare out the window at the trees, the darkness. "Why were you so obsessed with making me watch that video… and see Patrick, after, I mean, what you did to him?"

"After I punched and kicked him to death," Markus says. "I've already told you. You're a counsellor. You don't have the luxury of looking the other way. Nobody *should*, honestly. It's only the modern era that allows soft, weak cowards to plug their ears and close their eyes and sing *blah-blah-blah* any time they don't want to experience something. Once upon a time, a person would've seen ten corpses by their tenth birthday."

"And that was a *good* thing?"

"It's better than what we have now," he snaps, driving off the dirt track back onto an actual road. "If you were talking to a regular person today, and you mentioned one of, bloody hell, twenty or so topics, they'd have a meltdown. They'd be *seriously* psychologically affected. If you tell a dog lover that there's a dog theft epidemic in their area, many of them will visibly choose not to seriously process the information. And why, Katy? Because they *can*. They have the luxury of passing the responsibility onto somebody else. With their warm walls and their emergency services and their belief that all this, all this shit, roads and streets and shops and society, is real. But blood is real. Death is real. Animals are real."

"I'm not sure I understand what you mean," I say. "Animals are real… but society isn't?"

He laughs in that complicated way of his. "So you're counselling me now."

I almost retreat. But this is still my best plan of action, even if he's called it out. "It's one way to pass the time."

"Don't patronise me, at least," he says. "You know what I mean."

"I honestly don't. Maybe that choke robbed me of some of my brain cells."

He rolls his eyes. "It's not complicated. The modern woman is a deluded loser. The modern man is a weak loser."

"Deluded, how? Weak, how?"

Markus takes another turning. I spot a twenty-four-hour garage, lit up like a beacon, and then we're passed it. We're heading for the motorway again. "Have you seen the average man these days? Pot belly, skinny, pathetic arms. *Whiny*. The amount of men I hear whining is disgusting. Standing in line at the supermarket, pouting at their girlfriend because of some petty bullshit. And no violence in them at all."

"So you want men to be more violent?"

"It's the honest state of things. A man should be violent. He should be able to snap a bone or bite off a nose without flinching. It's the way we've been for all our history. Brutal and effective. Now, grown men play video games. They spend hours and hours watching porn. It's just a joke. You must see it."

"I agree there are problems," I reply. "But I don't think

turning every man into Conan the Barbarian is the way to go. I've been on the receiving end—"

"No, no, *no*." He slams his hand against the steering wheel. I cringe away. "You're about to completely misinterpret my point. You were going to talk about the rape, yes?"

"Y-yes," I mutter, hating that word, hating the fact it happened.

"But that's wrong. He did that to you precisely *because* the world is a non-violent, soft place. In a proper world, that instinct would've been beaten out of him the first time it reared its head. Or he'd be too capable and confident – through his mastery of violence – to ever think about doing something like that."

"So if we teach abusers to fight, they'll stop abusing."

"No. It's too late for that. But if *society*, as a whole, was much more violent, the world would be a better place. Certain states in America have it right. It's hard to misbehave when everybody's armed and willing to pull the trigger."

"So you think England should have *guns*?"

"Everything that's happened tonight, my dear Katy, and *this* is what shocks you most. Yes, I think England should have guns. The laws in our country are downright pathetic. You can't even use a weapon to defend yourself unless you happen upon it during the assault. If you pick up a brick on a building site and smash in a mugger's head, then, well, you might get off. But take a brick in your bag just in case… that's premeditation. Our ancestors would laugh if they saw how willingly we've let the government strip us of any way to defend ourselves."

I shake my head.

"You don't agree?" he says.

"Maybe I'm worried about voicing my opinion."

"If I hurt you, it won't be because of something you say."

I shouldn't believe him, but at least he's talking to me. And when he goes on his rants, he doesn't seem as composed. Maybe there's a way I can get closer to him through these discussions. Even the most poised person will accidentally share interesting details if kept talking long enough.

"Then I think your viewpoint is a little deluded," I say. "Arming people, making them more violent, would create more problems than it solves. You cited America. Surely I don't have to state the obvious."

"Yeah, yeah, school shootings."

"You say that like it's a small thing."

"An acceptable price."

I gasp. "Are you serious?"

"Half the children who were born, for most of our history, died before they were two years old. If it's a choice between freedom and life, I'll choose freedom every time."

"Were you not free, Markus? When you were a child?"

He pulls onto the motorway, quiet at this time of night. He's driving further away from Weston-super-Mare, heading toward Devon and Cornwall. "You'd like that, wouldn't you, Katy? That would tie this up in a neat bow for you."

"It's a simple que—"

"We're done talking."

I swallow a big lump of fear. But then I push past it. Try to, anyway, even as my voice wavers. "I thought you said you wouldn't hurt me for anything I say."

"True, but I can easily put you back in the boot."

I sit back, staring out the window again. I think I hit on something there. His childhood. Maybe if I keep digging, I'll get some answers. But there's no guarantee those answers will help me.

In the dark, for a moment, I think I see Patrick's corpse.

15

HIM

I shouldn't indulge so much in these discussions, especially after her little stunt. She's either refusing to get the point or trying to antagonise me, perhaps as a method of… of what? How does she think she's going to use any of this? She wanted to talk about my *childhood*, because of course she did. It's what unimaginative and boring people always want to do. Though, to be fair, I don't think Katy is boring. Or unimaginative.

All right, fine, but that doesn't mean this particular angle is warranted. I'm sure there are some things about Mum and Dad that led me to this path. I'm sure hearing the *noises* through the walls, and seeing Dad ignore it, and listening to his droning pointless prayers, and literally biting my tongue to stop from shouting that this is all wrong… Maybe she has a point.

But she's not going to get what she wants from me. Even now, as she stares mutely out the window, I can see her mind ticking away. Her neck is red from where I grabbed her. Her clothes are covered in filth. She looks so tiny… but also, somehow, stronger than when I first picked her up. A few layers of civilisation have been stripped away. Even if I ended this here, she'd be better equipped for life now.

It's been around half an hour since we last spoke. The motorway is peaceful.

"Do you want to try to guess where we're going?" I ask.

"Do you want me to guess?" she counters, still in counselling mode.

I decide to humour her for now. "Yes, I'd like that very much."

She folds her hands in her lap, then does a small side-to-side shift. I can imagine her doing it in her sessions. There's something about the movement that seems relaxing. She seems maternal, almost. "You clearly didn't choose me randomly. You went through the effort of creating your own taxi. You were obviously watching me for quite some time. The thing with Patrick—"

"The kidnapping and execution of a serial paedophile."

"Yes – that." She flinches, still trying to turn away from reality. "That wasn't specific to me. But clearly, you chose me for a reason. I imagine our next…" She pauses. "Activity will be more specific. But you're taking me away from home, away from my parents and friends."

"That's true. But that doesn't mean I'm taking you somewhere random."

"What do I get if I guess?"

"One of my winning smiles." I grin at her in the rear-view.

She smiles back. And, for a second, it seems real. It doesn't seem forced. To be fair to Katy, she's far more resilient than most people. Most regular women, after touching a corpse, smelling it, after being chased and choked, would be useless messes right now. Blubbering, moaning, basically begging for me to tie them up, gag their mouths, and store them in the boot. But, even if this is a performance, it's a testament to Katy's grit.

"I was hoping for something more concrete," she replies.

"Ah, yeah? Like what?"

"Some food. Some water. A change of clothes."

"I've got some cereal bars and bottled water in the glovebox. But first you have to guess."

"Am I allowed to ask any questions?"

I glance at the clock. It's just gone midnight. We'll be driving for at least another forty-five minutes. "Why not. I'll give you three."

She taps her chin, sticking her bottom lip out. I can see how some people would find this a very attractive pose. She's got a certain simple beauty when she's deep in thought. It's like all the mud and the filth has disappeared. "Are we going to see a friend of mine, either old or current?"

"No," I tell her.

"An enemy?"

"That depends on your perspective."

Another smile, this one playful. Stupidly – and weirdly, since I can usually control impulses like these – I find myself imagining what it would be like to be on a regular date with her. We could make small talk and she'd smile just like that, and we'd pretend that within a mile radius of where we sit sons and daughters and wives and husbands aren't being abused in every conceivable away.

"That isn't a very helpful answer."

"I don't know if they're your enemy or not. Like I said, it depends."

"Wait…" She narrows her eyes. "*They're*… so it's more than one person?"

"Is that your final question?" I ask.

"No, no." She shakes her head. "Does it have anything to do with… The Incident?"

"Ask me properly," I snap.

"My assault – my rape. Does it have anything to do with that?"

I focus on the road, picking up speed.

"Well?" she says urgently.

"You're a smart woman, Katy. I think you've already guessed."

16

KATY

Markus parks at the end of the cul-de-sac. The street is quiet: dead. When Markus kills the engine, we're sitting in complete darkness. I can just about make out the whites of his teeth as he beams at me from the front of the car.

I guessed right. It hit me when he said *they*. That, coupled with the general direction, gave me the hunch. Now, we're sitting across the street from Mr and Mrs Castle, the parents of the man who… who did what he did. They didn't attend the trial, but I remember hearing that the man was from Devon.

"This is a nice street," Markus says. "The average property price is three hundred thousand. Mr and Mrs Castle are a good, upstanding couple. They're both committed members of the local church. They *must* be good people, right, since this community still welcomes them, despite what their son did."

"Why are we here?" I ask.

"Haven't you ever wanted to confront them?"

"No," I answer honestly. "It's never crossed my mind."

"Pfft. That's because you've tried to bury this. But if you hadn't spent your life ignoring it, you'd want to confront them, wouldn't you?"

"Why would I?" I counter.

"Jesus Christ. You were just grilling me about my childhood. You were convinced it was my childhood that made me do this. What about *his*? Don't you want to know if there was something that led him to you?"

"No," I say, thinking of the couple sleeping in the house. They must be in their sixties at least, maybe seventies. *Just like Patrick…* yeah, okay, but the whole world can't be abusers of that sort. "It won't change anything. He's locked up now."

"Yeah, for eight years. He'll be out in five. This country… Well, Katy, you don't have a choice. You're going to knock on that door and *force* them to explain how they raised such a monster."

"Force… how?"

"Force your way into their home, into their minds, into their souls. You're going to scare the hell out of them."

"You're going to let me do this alone?"

"Pfft. Not *alone*. I'll be nearby. And if you decide to run again, you'll get more than a choke. I mean it – please take this seriously – if you run, and I manage to catch you without alerting anybody else, I'm going to cut off your pinkie finger. If you *do* alert somebody else, if the police are called, then I'll have to murder you."

I don't let the shock show on my face. It's more than just his words. It's the way he says them, as if it's a matter of fact.

"In the latter case," he goes on, "I'd have to make sure you were dead. This would involve an extremely brutal, quick method. I'm not sure exactly what I'd do, but I have a machete hidden somewhere in the car. I might use that. Oh, that reminds me…" He reaches into the glovebox, taking out a bottle of water and a cereal bar. "Do you want these before you head in there?"

"What do you expect me to do?" I ask.

"Scare them. Get them into the living room. Tell them you're here to learn why their loser, lowlife son did what he did."

"And if I do this?"

"Then you'll be physically unharmed, mostly anyway. More than I am." He gestures at his nose with a cereal bar. The design has a smiling dog on it. It seems so incredibly out of place here.

"But you won't let me go."

"No."

"Will you eventually?"

"I haven't decided yet," he snaps. "Do you want these or not?"

I almost tell him I'm not hungry, which is the truth. But I should eat. And my mouth is dry. If I'm going to have a chance to escape, I have to make the effort. "Yes, please."

I eat the cereal bar slowly.

"What's the problem?" Markus asks.

"It hurts when I swallow," I tell him, taking a small sip of water.

"Well, it hurts when I breathe through my nose, so we're even. Are you almost done?"

"You seem eager to get started," I note.

"*You* should be," he retorts.

"So just knock on the door, scare them, demand to be let inside?"

"Yes."

"And where will you be?"

"Watching from here," he says.

I look across the street at the house. It's at least twenty feet away. There's no way he's going to be able to hear what I'm saying. And if I run into the house, lock the door… no, he'll find a way in. But if I lock the door, grab a knife, barricade myself in the bathroom. I'll tell the police he has a gun. That'll get the

SWAT team out here, won't it? I wish I knew more about how law enforcement operates.

"Uh, okay," I mutter, reaching for the door. "You'll have to unlock the car."

He presses a button. There's a *click.* I'm still waiting for the punchline. Maybe his previous victims were far too terrified at this point to try anything. I probably *should* be. I don't consider myself particularly brave, but I'm not going to stop fighting.

"Remember what I said." He stares at me in the mirror. "Mess this up, you lose a finger. Ring the police, you lose your life."

I push open the door, and step into the cold air. My skin pricks as I walk across the street, pushing down the instinct of terror, the instinct that tells me to go along with this. But he's a man, flesh and blood and bone. It'll take him time to get into the house. To find me. And then he has to get past whatever weapon I can find.

I walk up the well-tended garden. It's difficult to blame Roger's parents when I see the care they've taken with the flowerbeds. A weird note, maybe, but it reminds me of my Mum's beloved garden. She only has a small plot, but she makes every inch count. I'd kill to be there now, in the sun, a book in my lap.

Before knocking on the door, I turn, feeling Markus' eyes on me. He's switched on the car's interior light. He sits there like a statue, mismatched eyes staring blankly. Turning back to the door, I raise my hand, take a breath.

Knock-knock-knock. It's so cold my knuckles hurt from the impact. Or perhaps that's the nerves winding through me. I expect a delay, but the door opens quickly. A tough-looking old man stands there in a smart shirt and chinos. His lean, sinewy arms are on display. He has a shaved head with a jagged scar across it.

He doesn't seem surprised. "What sort of time do you call this?"

My heart is thumping so, so hard. It's unhelpful, honestly. It almost causes me pain. "Please don't react to what I say next." I speak very slowly. "I'm being held hostage by a madman. See the taxi behind me? That's him. I'm…"

"I know who you are," he says. "Katy."

Ah, right. Of course he does. The trial. The publicity. The unfair shame. "He's brought me here to try and force me to hurt you, because of what your son did. Please, let me in. Try to look scared if you can. And then—"

It's not that he moves fast. It's the shock of it. Without warning, he turns his hips and fires off a stiff cross right into my gut. I gasp and cough, sputtering as I fall forward.

"I'm sorry," he says, and then pulls his hand back like he's going to hit me again.

No, screw that. I'm not giving him another free shot. I duck my head and spring at him. It's probably one of the messiest takedowns I've ever attempted. If he had any training, he'd wrap his arm around my throat and sink in a guillotine choke… which is as painful and effective as the name applies. But he's an old, confused-sounding man.

I hook his legs with my arms, drag him to the floor and then sit on top of him, squeezing my thighs, grabbing his wrists to control them. He groans and tries to sit up. I press all my weight against him, pinning him to the floor, wondering what to do from here. It's not as if I'm going to break his arm or choke him out.

"Stop," I snap, smashing his hand against the floor. "Fucking *stop*."

His struggling comes to an end, but I don't let his wrists go. He stares up at me with tears in his eyes. His nose is bleeding. I must've bumped into him during the takedown. A photo has fallen to the floor too.

When I see *his* smiling, sickening face through the cracked glass, I almost spit in the old man's face. They've got a photo of my assaulter hanging from the wall, even after what he did. Behind me, the door closes.

I don't turn. I don't have to. "Tut-tut," Markus says. "Now what did you say to dear Jonathan here to make him react like that, Katy?"

17

HIM

Katy doesn't turn, but a stiff jolt moves through her body. I'm impressed by how efficiently she was able to handle Jonathan. Of course, he's an elderly man, sixty-nine years of creaking bones and aching muscles. But he walks several miles a day and even does yoga. He's fit, and Katy was able to prove all that money spent on her class wasn't a *complete* waste.

I've closed the door behind me. This house is detached. Hopefully, none of the neighbours heard the scuffle. And even if they did, it would be simple enough to have Jonathan go to the door and claim he fell. But I doubt that will happen. The police have no part in this.

"Where's your wife, Jonathan?" I ask.

"She's taken a pill," Jonathan grunts from the floor, an offended note in his voice. He clearly dislikes the fact a woman half his size is holding him down.

"I told you I wanted to speak to you both tonight," I remind him. Katy jerks her head in my direction, clearly surprised.

"We can try to wake her, but I doubt she'll be any good to you."

I bite down, wondering if he's trying some trick. Reaching

into my pocket, I take out a few zip ties and kneel beside them. "Don't move," I snap, talking to them both. I zip-tie their wrists together, and then grab Jonathan's leg, extend it, and zip-tie his ankle to the heater pipe.

"Wait here," I say, and then almost laugh. It's not like they're going anywhere.

Heading upstairs, I find the Castle's bedroom. Marcy is on her side, her lined face looking far too peaceful considering the monster she unleashed into the world. She doesn't even stir as I zip-tie her ankles to the bedposts—making sure to use the correct zip ties; not the ones I treated to test Katy—then quickly search the room for a phone. There's nothing.

"You're lucky," I tell her motionless body. "Or unlucky, depending on how this goes. I hope you have a loud shout. Your husband may not be around to cut you loose."

I'm not sure why I say any of this. It's not as if it gives me a thrill. Or maybe that's a lie. Maybe I'm just a monster trying to convince myself otherwise. Or maybe I don't give a single shit about what or why or how I am.

Walking downstairs, I find the happy couple still intertwined.

"Remember what I told you," I mutter, as I kneel and cut the ties loose with my sharp, weighty blade. "Katy? Are you listening?"

She sniffles, her head pushes against Jonathan's chest. "I-I-I…"

"Don't start that stuttering nonsense," I say. "I warned you. You ignored me. You should psychologically prepare yourself for losing a pinkie finger. I'll even let you choose which hand."

"Please," she says, and then she does something very, very stupid. Throwing her head back, she starts screaming like an idiot. She only manages to do it for half a second until my hand is clamped over her mouth. I squeeze hard. I feel her jaw straining under the force I apply. She stops right away.

"Now you don't get a choice," I tell her. "Now, you're losing both. If you scream again, it's a whole hand."

Grabbing a big bunch of her hair, I guide her to her feet. She gasps and struggles as I drag her into the living room. There are more photos of their evil son in here. The freaks.

"Jonathan." I glance over at him lurking in the doorway, knowing better than to try and stop me. "Get a first-aid kit. And some whisky."

He turns, trembling slightly, disappears into the house. I'm aware this could all end here, if Jonathan wasn't such a coward. A secret phone call, a plea for help. But he thinks, if he complies, he'll survive this. They always think that. When I push Katy onto the sofa, she glares up at me. It's like she's getting herself ready for another attack. It's in her body language, the way she leans forward, fists clenched.

"I warned you," I tell her. "Stop pouting at me."

"So you're in this together. You and *them*."

"I'm not in anything with them. They're part of this because I made them a part of it. It wasn't even difficult. A few threats, a few phone calls, showing up a few times while they slept. I told them we'd be coming. I told them to go along with it, if you did as I asked… which you really, really should have, Katy."

"Why don't you just get this over with," she hisses.

I toss my blade from hand to hand. "You're missing the point. This is a reasonable punishment for a mistake you made. Well, two mistakes. Disobeying me and screaming."

Jonathan returns with what I asked, places it on the coffee table, then sits on the armchair with his hands crossed. He's trying to look so damn dignified: middle-upper class, civilised and put upon. Katy looks at him… and I see it: a flash of something wrong. *Sick*. I'm far too good at reading people to be a psychopath. The look is one of pity.

"Look around this room," I growl, nudging Katy's foot with

mine. "Look at the photos." She stares down at her feet. It pains me to have to do this, but she's making it so difficult. I put the knife against her throat, use it to lift her chin. "I said *look*."

She looks across the room at the glass display cabinet. Not only is there a photo of their mongrel son in there, it's the *biggest* one, taking pride of place. And it's not even a photo of when he was a child, as if they wanted to remember better times. "That was taken in the prison chapel," I tell Katy. "They talk to their son all the time, don't you, Jonathan?"

Jonathan gets all misty-eyed, shivering as he looks up at me. The cowardice reeks. He's so pathetic, it makes me feel weaker just being close to him. "Yes," he says quietly.

"I'm looking," Katy says. "Now what?"

"Well… how do you feel?"

"I feel like I'm psychologically preparing myself to lose two fingers."

I step away, gesture with the knife. "Don't worry about that right now."

She laughs humourlessly, looking down at the muddy carpet, then at Jonathan, also streaked in mud from the scuffle. The room stinks of old people and filth. "I don't know how I can't worry about it, honestly."

"I'm interested in how you feel about the fact they're proudly displaying photos of your rapist."

"How do you *think* I feel?" she snaps, far more fight than Jonathan has. It's bothersome that she disobeyed me, obviously, but at least she's got some fire in her.

"I'm asking you."

She grits her teeth. Her eyes are watering. She's trying not to cry. I'll never understand how a person can allow themselves to simply cry when their world is all twisted up. Instead of doing something useful, instead of fighting or reasoning, they leak from their eyes. Pathetic. But at least she's trying *not* to.

"How about this?" I go on. "I'll make you a deal. If you humour me – and if you agree to do something for me before we leave here tonight – you get to keep your fingers."

"Do what?" she asks.

"Nah-uh. You have to agree now."

"But it might be something worse than losing my fingers."

"Maybe. But it's a risk you'll have to take."

Her face tells an entire story, future possible pain versus present, guaranteed agony. "Fine," she says after a pause. "It makes me sick. It makes me angry. They shouldn't have photos of him on the wall. They shouldn't have photos of him *anywhere*."

"Jonathan, why don't you sit next to Katy." It's not a question, and the man moves immediately. I wink at Katy. "It's like a couple's counselling session." She doesn't seem to get the joke.

Once Jonathan and Katy are sat together, the old man dabs at his busted nose with a piece of tissue paper. "Liam, please," he whispers.

"Liam?" Katy says. "Oh – right – is anything real about you, Markus?"

I smirk. "I'm obviously not going to give you my real name. Don't be naïve. Now, tell Jonathan how you feel."

"I just did."

"No, you told *me*."

She grits her teeth, looking like she's getting ready for another scrap. But then she visibly comes to her senses, turns, looks at Jonathan. "You know what your son did."

"Yes," Jonathan said.

"But you have photos of him up everywhere anyway."

Jonathan dabs at his nose again. "Yes, we do."

"Well…" Oh, this is good. She leans forward, looks at him with murderous hate in her eyes. "Why would you do that? Why would you think that's acceptable? He… he assaulted me."

"Use plain English," I cut in.

Katy flinches. I can see the desire to retreat. It's like an aura. It's all around her, the need to look away, to never bravely and bluntly face her hell. But then she goes on. "Your son raped me. You *know* he raped me."

"Well," I snap, after a pause. "Aren't you going to respond, Jonathan?"

"God have mercy," he says.

"*No*." I slam my foot on the floor, far too loudly. But the street doesn't seem to be stirring. "Don't start with that God shit. He has no place here. Talk to Katy. You owe her that much, at least."

Jonathan looks at Katy. There's an obvious violent intent in him. It's difficult to pinpoint exactly what it is about him, but he didn't like being manhandled by a woman. I hope Katy can sense this too; it'll make the end of our visit much easier. "He repented in prison," Jonathan says. "He's found God. He's been born again. He's not the same man who committed those wicked sins."

"You have got to be shitting me."

I laugh. A *real* laugh. "That's exactly what I said, Katy. Didn't I? Tell her."

Jonathan nods, but he doesn't see the humour in it.

"So he just *repented*? And that was good enough for you?"

Jonathan glances at me.

"You can talk about God if it's in this context," I tell him. "Just don't start that self-pitying bleating. It's insufferable. And anyway, if your god was real, I wouldn't be here."

"It took a lot of prayers," Jonathan mutters. I experience a note of satisfaction when Jonathan leans *away* from Katy. He must be able to sense how badly she wants to hurt him. "It took many, many conversations with our priest. But our son's soul was cleaned when he experienced his second birth."

I tap my knife against my knee, waiting for Katy to speak. She looks understandably bothered by Jonathan's insane statement.

"Prayers," she says after a long pause, making the word as vicious as it deserves. "Do you understand what he did to me?"

"I was at the trial," Jonathan says, with that annoying, up-his-own-arse tone a lot of men his age get. They think because they've achieved the stunningly easy feat of reaching old age in a first-world country that they are in some way better than everybody else.

"So you heard the details," Katy says. "About what he did."

Jonathan hesitates, looks at me, the knife. It's like he'd rather take the blade than have to hear, in precise detail, the nature of his son's evil.

"*Did you hear what he did*?" Katy snaps, not *quite* a shout. This is so much better than before. She looks like she's ready to hurt the sad sack of bones.

"I couldn't go to the trial, it was too painful," Jonathan finally admits.

"Enlighten him, Katy," I say.

18

KATY

This is so… No, I won't go there. Surreal or not, it's happening. My aching body tells me we're in the real world. I know what Markus – or whatever his name is – is trying to get me to do. He wants me to hate this man, maybe even hurt him. I made a deal to *do something* before we leave. It's not difficult to figure out what. Or, at least, the general direction it will take.

But I didn't expect this rage. Real and boiling, it makes me want to tackle the old man again. It's the way he looks at me… almost like it's *my* fault. Markus has just told me to enlighten him, but I don't think I can.

"He knows what happened," I say.

"You heard him," Markus counters, tossing his knife from hand to hand, the motion like the swinging pendulum of a clock. "He ran, like a coward. He couldn't stomach the details. How does that make you feel, knowing he's forgiven his rapist son and he couldn't even listen to what exactly happened?"

Markus is manipulating me… and it's working. It would be better not to be conscious of the fact. But, with a degree of detachment, I can watch it play out. Markus is manoeuvring me into place, making me the resentful victim. But Jonathan doesn't even look *ashamed*.

"You have to know the details of the case," I snap.

Jonathan hesitates. "I… know enough."

"Tell him in detail. This will be good for you. You can't hide from it forever. You'll never be able to heal. He's not going to hurt you." I wonder if Markus sees the irony in his reassurance. "And you're not going to hurt yourself. It's over. These are just words."

"It's more than that," I say.

"You have to tell him, Katy. Just try."

I take a breath, reminding myself I could be short two fingers right now. It's only playing this game that has delayed that. I tried it my way, and it just made it worse. And they're just *words*.

Keeping my gaze focused on Jonathan, I speak slowly. "It was a regular day. I was walking home through the park. I decided to go the long way, through the mini wooded area. I remember there was this one squirrel who seemed to be following me. I stopped, took some photos, kept on my way…"

The next part makes me shudder. It always does, whether it comes to me when I'm awake or asleep. Sleep is the worst. I'll tremble myself awake, then lie there, half in the real world and half in the memory, unable to move. "Then a sweaty hand was over my mouth. I remember how he – how he…"

"Don't break down," Markus says. "You can do this. You're doing so well."

Jonathan's placid, seemingly unbothered expression is what drives me on. He's clearly trying not to hear my words. On the surface, he's listening. But I've counselled enough people to know when somebody's attempting to tune me out.

"I remember how he tuh-tasted," I force myself to say. "Like oil. Tobacco. Sweat. It was so disgusting. The attack was so much more violent than I ever imagined."

In my previous martial art, we'd practised what to do if a man grabbed us. In bright, air-conditioned rooms, instructors had gently laid their hands on our heads, giving us ample time to karate chop the offending limb away and spring into a choreographed sequence. Real life was more like a gunshot to the chest.

"Before I could react – before I could *think* about reacting – I was in the duh-duh…"

"Keep. Going." Markus taps the knife against his teeth; it's a weird and somewhat demonic gesture.

"Dirt," I say, then drag in a huge breath like I've lifted a weight. "The dirt was scratching against my neck. It was summer. The mud was dry. I remember how strong his hands felt on my knickers."

Jonathan *still* isn't reacting. He's got his hands folded. He reminds me of the countless older men I've encountered in my life, whether it be through work or incidentally. I can almost hear his thoughts. *When the silly girl is done talking, we can get onto the truly important matters…*

"I spit in his face. He laughed. Your son *laughed*." I slam my hand down on the sofa between me and Jonathan, causing him to flinch… then get angry, offended. He wants to hurt me. All he's thinking about is how I took his old, pathetic arse down. "He laughed and said something. Do you know what it was?"

I feel as if I'm there now, staring up at him, the deranged glee. "I could tell he'd been waiting a long time for this. He was looking at me like it was Christmas morning. I was his present. *Do you know what he said*?"

Leaning closer to Jonathan, I search for a reaction. I can feel Markus staring. Feel his approval. I don't need it, don't want it. Do I? What sort of freak would I be if I wanted that? Jonathan is making this too damn hard.

"She asked you a question," Markus grunts.

"No," Jonathan replies, as though he'll only speak if another man commands him to.

I take a moment to prepare myself. After tonight, this should be easy. It's not. "He said, *'I'm going to ruin your little hole first and then I'm going to fuck your ass like the horny slut you are.'*" I'm almost crying again. But screw that. I wish I was the one holding the knife. "Your son was smiling as he said that, just so you know. My *little* hole. He was talking to me like I was a child. And, as he… did what he did—"

"No, Katy," Markus snaps.

"As he raped me!" I explode. "He talked to me like I was a child. *Good girl*. Sick shit like that. That's what your son did. But what? He gets to say a few prayers, splash around in some water, and it doesn't matter anymore?"

Jonathan doesn't say anything, just watches me. I'm not sure what to do. I want to hit him, honestly. I was on top of him just minutes ago. I could've grabbed his arm, broken it, or tried to. Or just hit him over and over until his face was unrecognisable. I've got a template now; I'll be as savage as Markus was with Patrick in that storage building.

"What now?" Jonathan finally says.

"That's… it?" I reply. "You don't have anything to say?"

"I've said everything I need to." He sits up, Mr Fucking Dignified. "My son made his mistakes. But he repented and in the eyes of the…"

He trails off when, almost soundlessly, Markus walks over and places the knife against his throat.

Markus looks down at me. "Jonathan doesn't care what his son did. He doesn't even care about his son. All he cares about is his church. After your rape, after the trial, they were outcasted for a short time. But then his son had his come-to-Jesus moment, and they were able to weasel their way back in. You'll never get a reaction out of him because he simply doesn't care. As long as he has his church fayres and bake sales and choir and all that shit, he's happy to let his son abuse a thousand women, ten thousand."

"Why did you bring me here, then?" I ask. "Why are you doing any of this?"

"Pfft. You know I'm not going to answer *that*. But as for your first question… because I want you to understand. Some people are too sick to be cured. You could show him a video and he *still* wouldn't care. Tell her, Jonathan…" He pushes the knife against the old man's throat more deliberately, causing him to lean away. "Be honest."

"I just want what's best for my wife."

"Be *honest*. I won't ask you again."

"Well… of course I love my church. I love the community. I won't be ashamed of that."

"Even if you know what your son did was wrong, downright evil. Even if you know that any decent father would disown the little toerag. Even if you know that your son changed this woman's life forever. His choice, his perversion, his sin… But oh, at least you get to go to the bake sale… It's pathetic."

Jonathan cringes away from the knife, tears appearing in his eyes, blinking as he tries to fight them away. A jolt of pity tries to enter my mind. I feel it like a poison. But then the anger rushes in. I can just see him with his church pals, all of them muttering about his son the rapist, how he erred, how he's on the path now, amen.

Markus turns to me, holding the knife in place. "Do you have any other questions for him?"

Telling myself I'm doing this to play the game – not because I want to, not because it's bringing me a weird sense of satisfaction – I say, "What did you do to him to make him so messed up? What sort of twisted childhood did he have? I know not everything starts in childhood, but this… something must've happened. You must have some sort of explanation."

"I did my best," Jonathan says.

"Don't play dumb." Markus prods him with the blade. A drop of blood slides down his neck. "She's asking if you diddled the boy. Or hit him. Or cheated on your wife with him in the same room. The sort of sick shit that turns little boys into sick shits."

"Nothing like that!" Jonathan snaps. "We always supported him, loved him."

"Maybe he was abused elsewhere," Markus muses. "Or perhaps you're lying. We don't have the time to get to the bottom of it. We've hung around long enough. Okay, Katy, are you ready for your challenge?"

I try to steel myself for whatever happens next. So far, shock has ruled me, from the moment I got in the taxi, to Patrick, and then the sucker punch from Jonathan. Now, I promise myself, nothing will shock me.

"Yes," I say.

"All you have to do is… say yes." Markus grins. "Just say yes and I will kill this man right here."

"And if I say no, you're going to make good on your original threat."

"You'll have to be punished," Markus says, as though it's the most reasonable thing in the world. "But I think this is a very fair deal."

"You promised." *Now* Jonathan starts showing some emotion. He blubbers, tears falling down his cheeks like the blood down his wrinkled neck. "Do what you said – and you'd leave us be. You *promised*!"

"Stop whining," Markus says, his voice flat and emotionless. Somehow, that's scarier than when he's pretending to be human. "Yes or no, Katy? We haven't got all night."

Pity tries to twist through me like a constricting snake. It tries to twist me up. There's too much empathy in me for a night like this. The fact is, Jonathan probably isn't an evil man. Markus is right – his son could've experienced the malforming hell elsewhere. Jonathan could simply be an elderly man trying to make his way in the world.

That probably makes the speed of my answer all the worse. It's no choice at all really. It's self-preservation. That's my excuse. But really, I wonder if it's the white-hot rage in my belly… in my sex, in my ass, in all the places his son claimed. His sick, fucked-up son. And now they're singing *choir* songs.

"Yes," I say. "Fucking kill him!"

19

HIM

Oh, wow. Now *this* is downright delicious. If men like me were made to feast on regular people's emotions, this is a banquet. Katy loses her cool, shouts at me to kill Jonathan. In this moment, she's pure, *real*. She's not another fleshy sack dragging itself over the scaffolding of civilisation. She has a definite, gleaming purpose.

"Nuh-no," Jonathan whines. "You can't—"

Grabbing the back of his head with one hand, I use the leverage, and my own strength, to push the blade firmly into him. He croaks and his body starts to convulse. One hand strikes at the blade with surprising strength. I control his wrist as he thrashes onto the floor, blood pissing everywhere.

Katy stands up instinctively, covers her mouth. It's what she asked for… and she looks shocked. How disappointing. But I saw the real her, just for a moment. We'll get there again.

"Don't run," I tell her when she turns toward the door. At the same time, I stab Jonathan in the mouth, feeling the blade scrape against his teeth before I drive it down his throat. It's the most efficient way, in my opinion. He'll choke before he bleeds out. "Remember – a whole hand otherwise."

Katy makes a straitjacket of her arms, wrapping them around herself, cringing against the wall.

"You asked for this," I tell her, standing and wiping the knife on my trousers, purposefully a dark colour since I knew tonight would get messy. Still, they reek of the mess I made with Patrick. It'll be time to change soon. "Right. We better go. We've made far too much noise."

Jonathan shivers from the floor. Well, his body does. His soul, if there is such a thing, is gone now.

"Katy, stop shaking. I did what you *told* me to do."

"It wasn't much of a choice," she whispers.

"Nah-uh. Don't rewrite history. You wanted it."

Tucking the knife into my waistband, I take Katy's arm and lead her into the hallway. Looking up the stairs, I wonder if I should go upstairs and finish the job. Marcy is likely to talk about the strange man who's been visiting their home, my voice, my mannerisms, the times of my visit.

"I'm going to have to zip-tie and gag you for a minute."

"Why?"

I drive her to the floor with a firm grip on her arm. She crumples under the pressure. "Why do you think?"

I zip-tie her to the radiator—using *her* zip ties, wondering if and when she'll try—then go into the kitchen and quickly return with a kitchen towel. Stuffing that into her mouth, I jog up the stairs.

Once that business is handled, I take Katy back to the car, throw her into the backseat. I pull away quickly, the tyres screeching on the road. Then I drive at a regular speed, no rush, taking a roundabout route that has the fewest CCTV cameras.

"How many people are going to die tonight?" Katy asks quietly.

"Don't take the moral high ground now."

"You killed the old lady too."

"That old lady called you a *lying slut* to my face several times. She was even more vicious than Jonathan about it, honestly. And anyway, you *wanted* me to kill them. But now, to save your misguided morality, you want to pretend I forced you. Fine. If it makes you feel better, go ahead. Just be thankful you've got all your fingers."

She pushes her face against the window.

"I'm proud of you," I say, when she just sits there, sulking.

"Why are you so desperate to talk?" she asks.

"I know it was hard for you," I go on, ignoring her counsellor's fishline. "To explain in detail. The memories. The tastes. But if you live through this, you'll be grateful."

"Do you honestly believe that?" she asks.

If it makes her talk, I'll play her game, then. She's clearly determined to switch the focus onto me. "Yes."

"So you think that kidnapping an innocent person and exposing them to extreme violence is somehow a moral good."

"*Fucking kill him!*" I yell, imitating her voice. Her eyes snap open wide. It's like she's just heard a recording of herself. I chuckle. "I know. I could be on *Britain's Got Talent*. Best impressionist in the country, I am, Katy."

"I lost my temper." She keeps sulking. "I didn't…"

"What? Want me to kill him?" Instead of taking the motorway, I turn down a country road, the lights cutting across the tall hedges and the fields beyond. "We both know that's a lie. For one beautiful second, you showed me who you really are. If you were born in a different era, one not so determined to file down any edge that seemed slightly too rough, you would've painted yourself in his blood and *danced*."

She pushes her face against the window again, determined not to speak to me.

"I thought you were going to interrogate me on the counsellor's chair, Katy?"

"There's no point. All you do is try to turn it around on me. You think you're being clever. But you're not. You're being predictable."

She speaks in a detached tone, making me wonder if this is genuine, not a ploy of some kind. Maybe she's so beaten down by this experience that she thinks talking to me in this manner is acceptable. But, perhaps strangely, I don't feel the urge to discipline her. She showed herself to me. That violent flash. *Fucking kill him*.

"Okay, then," I reply. "Counsel me. I'll be honest."

She sits forward, staring at me in the rear-view, her face caked in mud and blood. "So you're going to tell me the truth."

"Generally speaking, that's what honesty means."

"How can I believe you?"

"Because I don't care. I've never cared. It's like a superpower. If the police arrest me tomorrow, I'll go to prison, read books, workout. I'm not scared of it. If the hard men in there try to hurt me, I'll hurt them. I'll find ways to exploit the weaker inmates. But first… why don't we get cleaned up? I've got water and spare clothes in the boot. We both stink."

She nods slowly. "I'd like that."

"But don't try anything," I warn her.

"Don't worry. I've learned my lesson."

20

KATY

As Markus or whatever his name is pulls the car up at the side of the road – driving over a muddy track so we're under the cover of trees – I wonder if it's true… If I've really learned my lesson. Maybe I'd be an idiot to try to escape again. I saw how efficiently he killed Jonathan, like it was nothing.

"You're going to need to strip," Markus says. "Then we'll scrub you down, towel you off, and get you changed."

"You want me to get naked."

"I know it's going to be psychologically difficult for you. But I swear, I'm not interested in you in *that* way. I don't pretend to be a good man, but forcing myself on a woman… it's simply not in my DNA. In fact, I think sexuality has become filthy in recent years."

"I'm not sure I can undress for you," I tell him.

"Men have turned into wild dogs. They always *were* dogs. But society has allowed them to rut and roll and then move on, with the woman sitting there, leaking, trying to convince herself she had a good time too, trying to convince herself she wasn't just used. I have no interest in using another human being."

This statement is so deluded, I think he's joking at first.

"Isn't that what you're doing with me?" I counter, knowing I could be risking a lot by talking back. I have to ignore this strange note of intimacy I feel between us… no, not *intimacy.* But closeness. Shared experience. Almost like we're a team. It's messed up.

"I'm not using you. I'm helping you. If it wasn't for your petty little escape attempts, you wouldn't even be injured. Take your clothes off, Katy. Let's get this over with."

"How can I—"

He slams his hand on the steering wheel. "Surely you understand, if I wanted to do *that*, I could've done it dozens of times already. It would be stunningly simple. Drag you from the car – tackle you to the ground—"

"Okay, okay," I cut in, before he starts going into detail. "Fine. Just don't look, please."

"I've seen it all before," he replies.

I shudder. "No you haven't."

"You leave your hallway curtains open. Sometimes, when you're getting ready, or before a shower, you'll walk naked through your flat. I've seen your body."

"How long have you been watching me?" I ask.

"Nah-uh. We haven't begun our counselling session yet. Strip."

"What if I'd rather stay dirty?"

"You stink. I stink. And if we need to go somewhere public, we can't look like this."

I try not to let too much hope into my should-know-better heart when he says that. If we go into a public place, there's a far better chance of escape… or of me getting somebody else killed. A child abuser and the elderly parents of my rapist, perhaps I can handle that. But some innocent young woman working the night shift at a garage?

Slowly, I start taking off my clothes. It's too dark for Markus to be able to see. I can only make out his outline. But I know he could switch on the lights, see me exposed.

"That was good work on Jonathan, by the way," he says. "When you took him down and controlled him. Your teachers would be proud."

"He was an old man."

"He's a *man*. You're a *woman*. It doesn't matter how old he was. He was fit for his age. The fact you were able to handle yourself says a lot. If their deranged son pounced on you now, I think it would go differently."

Again, I ignore that weird, confusing sense of camaraderie. The compliment, I have to tell myself, does nothing for me. Finally, I wriggle out of my knickers, sitting naked in the back of the car.

"I've undressed," I tell him.

"I'm going to open the back door. You can stand on your old clothes. I'll give you a sponge. Do your best to scrub yourself down. It's going to be cold. Very cold. But I can put the heating on when we're done."

"Then what?" I ask.

"You can ask all the questions you want as we drive."

"But where are we going next?"

"Tut-tut. Don't make me threaten you again."

He opens the door, his tall, wide silhouette walking to the rear door. Our stops so far make it clear that I need to figure out a way to prevent us reaching our next one. If the car broke down… would that be better? It would be a delay, at least. Next time I get a chance, if I stun him for a moment, I'll have to be far, far more brutal. I'll have to rake his eyes out of his head. I'll have to kill him.

Opening my door, he grunts, "Out."

I place my clothes on the muddy ground, stand on them, shivering immediately as a cold wind slices across.

"Do I need to zip-tie you when I get the water?" he says.

"Where am I going to run?"

"You seem to be understanding your situation a little better now."

He walks to the boot. It's so dark, I'm able to kneel down without him noticing. I'm not sure what I'm doing, exactly. It's like instinct is guiding me. Disable the car – then what? We're in the middle of nowhere. But this tour has to stop. Maybe his next *test* will be to see if I'll hurt a child or something depraved like that. I can't let his bullshit morality talk twist me up.

Markus returns holding a large bottle of water. He hands me a sponge.

"Get ready to scrub," he says. "And get ready to shiver."

I gasp when the water begins to flow over me. It's not much of a shower, but I scrub my skin raw, telling myself I can scrub away what happened at the house. I wanted that old man to die. It excited me. I hungered for it. I keep scrubbing even when I feel my skin burning.

Finally, the water stops flowing. "I'll get you a towel," Markus says.

"Such a gentleman," I reply.

I didn't plan on saying that. What the hell is wrong with me? But it must be my instinct to escape, trying to win his trust, all part of the plan. He chuckles, and it sounds genuine. But he also sounded like a real chatty cab driver when he first picked me up, so it doesn't matter how he *sounds*.

"Only the best for you," he says, returning to the boot.

"You came prepared," I say, when he hands me the towel.

"You've seen how messy this can get. But I didn't plan on a run through a muddy field."

"I'm sorry," I whisper, rubbing myself down.

"For trying to escape? For trying to fight? Honestly, Katy,

you're doing far better than every other woman I've ever seen in your situation."

"Seen," I repeat. "That's an interesting way to phrase it."

"How so?"

"It absolves you of responsibility. You didn't just *see* them, did you?" If he's done this before… there's no way he let those women go. He might talk big about prison, but nobody *wants* to go there. "You kidnapped them."

"Fair enough. But the point stands. You're doing great. Once you're dressed, I'm going to need to lock you in the car."

"I'm as dry as I'm going to get," I tell him.

He goes to the back again, returning with a bundle of clothes. "You're a size ten, right?"

"How do you know that?"

"I've been in your flat," he says casually, as if it's the most normal thing in the world.

"Why?" I say, hoping to hide my reaction of pure, visceral disgust.

"I'm interested in you. You can tell a lot about a person by the way they live. Take you, Katy. You present an orderly image to the world. You're never late. You're professional. But on the floor next to your bed… it's like a war zone. Clothes strewn everywhere. It's as if you think you can contain the chaos of life to those two square metres."

"How profound," I mutter, pulling on the hoodie.

"Don't get bitter with me," he snaps.

What else am I supposed to do, *thank* him for snooping around my flat? I quickly pull on the boxer-brief-style underwear and the tracksuit bottoms, relieved Markus kept to his word and didn't try anything sexual with me. *Yet*, anyway. I can't let myself fall into the trap of believing he's even a little bit good.

"Are you done?" he says.

"Yeah."

"Okay, get in the car."

I climb into the backseat. He closes the door, locks it, leaving me to wrap my arms around myself and shudder as the cold clings to me. He approaches washing himself in the same way he approaches everything, in the most efficient manner possible. When he's done, he carries the clothes to the back of the car. Returning to the driver's seat, he switches on the heating and the interior light.

He winks at me in the rear-view. "All better now?"

"I wouldn't say *all* better."

He shrugs. "It's like you're determined to be in a bad mood."

What sort of mood am I *supposed* to be in? It's such a ludicrous thing for him to say.

"Are you ready to have a talk with me, Markus?"

"Uh-oh. Your tone's changed. You're in counselling mode now, I can tell."

"Well?"

"Fine. But we're going one-for-one. You ask. I ask. The first person to lie loses."

"How will I know if you're lying? How will you know if I am?"

"I can always tell," he says. "And you should be able to, too. It's your job. Right. Go on. Ask away while we dry off."

This might be completely pointless. He could easily lie to me, probably *will* lie to me.

"How many women have you killed?" I ask.

21

HIM

I don't like her question one bit. She puts emphasis on *killed*, whether she realises it or not. She could've asked me anything as her first question, but she chose that, as if she wants to frame me as the bad guy from the outset. But I told her I'd be honest. I won't break that rule until she does. It's oddly pleasant with the heating running, out here in the middle of nowhere, only the stars watching.

"A few," I tell her. "More than a few."

She does a good job at hiding her reaction, but she can't defeat the micro expressions, the tightening at the corners of her mouth and eyes. "Why?"

"Nah-uh…"

"Oh, okay." She nods. "Your turn, then."

"How many men have you slept with?" I ask.

She flinches. "What does that have to do with anything?"

"It says a lot about a woman."

"How's that?"

"You're forgetting our rule."

"I'm curious."

"Isn't it obvious?" I say. "If a woman has slept with, say, more than fifty men, there's a high probability she was sexually abused at some point during her development. Now she uses promiscuity as her shield. That's the best-case scenario. The worst-case is that these poor women have bought into the lie that sex can be as casual for them as it can for men. And now they're ruined. Their minds are shattered. They're broken. You don't seem broken, Katy, but I'd like to be sure."

"I've slept with nine men," she snaps. "Not that it means anything."

"As a student of the mind, you seem determined to be ignorant about very straightforward things."

"My turn… why did you kill those women?"

I adjust the heating, making it even warmer. In preparation for this night, I adapted my sleeping pattern over a two-week period. There's no danger of me passing out. But Katy looks a little spacey.

"Would you like a case-by-case breakdown?"

"Sure."

"The first woman I killed was a mistake. She tried to run, like you did, but it was new territory to me and I overreacted. I grabbed her too hard, dragged her to the car… I accidentally choked her out on the way. The others were more or less the same – the experiments were over. They failed. I didn't want to risk them talking to the police."

She swallows, but again, she does a decent job at hiding her mammalian response. Far better than the others when the prospect of their murders emerged.

"Remember our deal," I tell her. "You have to be honest."

"I have been."

"But you might be tempted to lie when I ask my next question." I pause, then say, "When we were in Jonathan's house, and I gave you power over his life, did it excite you?"

She clasps her hands together, fidgeting. "Define *excite*."

"Don't mess me around."

"I'm serious. It's a broad term."

"Did you badly want me to kill him? Did you feel a sense of urgency? Did it feel like the right thing to do?"

She doesn't answer for a long time. I let her torture herself with the silence. It's like I can watch the battle raging behind her eyes. For many people, this would be a simple *yes*. But Katy has a perception of herself as an upstanding member of this lofty civilisation. People like that don't bay for blood.

"Yes," she finally says.

"Well done. I can tell that was difficult for you. Your turn."

"Is there a chance I will live through this night?"

"Yes," I tell her.

"Is it a big chance?" She bites down, a small smile. "Sorry."

If I cared for such things, I might brand her *cute* right now. There's something about her apology that… does something to me. It's curious and new. "If you had the power to kill me now, would you do it?"

"No," she says.

I almost laugh, but she seems so sincere. She's lying, though. She has to be. I've stalked her, violated her privacy, kidnapped her, exposed her to the kind of brutality most people can't even envision in their living-in-a-bubble lives.

"Even after everything I've done?"

"I don't want to kill anybody," she says, and I believe her. The idiot. She *should* want to kill me. "I know I had my… lapse with Jonathan. I was angry. I was stressed. But if I'm able to make a real decision, I'd never choose to take somebody's life."

"That's incredibly naïve," I tell her.

She shrugs. "Maybe it is. But if more people thought like me, the world would be a far better place. My turn, remember? Why do you hate women so much?"

"I don't hate them," I reply. "I love women. I think they're far superior to men in most respects. They're more empathetic. They're kinder. They're more honest. They're far more selfless."

"But…"

"I know. I kidnap them. I kill them. Confusing, isn't it?"

"Then maybe you could explain your thinking behind it."

"First—"

"Your turn. Yeah."

"Have you ever been in love?"

"Yes, I had a boyfriend in my early twenties. But I ended things. By the time I regretted it, it was too late. He has a wife and kids now."

"Another blight for the modern woman. Far too many options. Far too many silly thoughts in your head, filling you up with dreams of grandeur. It's the *Eat, Pray, Love* mentality. A joke. Go into the world – find yourself… then come back to a lonely flat filled with cats and wine bottles and the sound of your own sobbing."

She ignores me, leaps straight into her question. "Can you explain, if you don't hate women, why you kidnap them?"

Even though she might've lied to me – when she said she wouldn't kill me if she had the chance – I decide to tell her the truth. "My father was a drunk and an absurdly religious man. He was also my mother's pimp. My mother's feminine attributes, her empathy, her loyalty, her kindness, they all worked against her. She was too kind to do what she should've done. Kill the bastard. So now, I make that right. I help women be stronger."

"But you haven't."

"*Yet*," I tell her. "So far, you're giving me hope."

"There are some who might say you're using this as an excuse. If you can establish some kind of moral framework around your actions, then you don't have to feel guilty. But at the end of the day, it comes down to this… you *like* it."

"Those people would be wrong," I say. "Guilt doesn't bother me. I don't feel it. I don't feel much. We're done with this."

"Have I upset you?" she asks, with a smirk, a *smirk* after everything that's happened. I have to give it to her. She's impressive.

"Ha, ha, ha." I turn the key, the engine growling to life.

22

KATY

He talks about murder so casually. Perhaps it's a mistake, but I believe what he's said. He killed them because they didn't show him the results he wanted to see. If he's being honest about his mum, then he obviously wants to turn a woman into the fierce, capable, callous person she would've needed to be to escape his father. That's something. A lifeline. Make myself tough for whatever happens next.

We join a country road, then cut through a village, before he notices the flat tyre.

"Fuck's sake," he grumbles. "This is honestly the last thing we need."

"Have you got a spare?" I ask.

"No." From the way he answers – gritted teeth, sighing after – I can tell he's annoyed with himself. The man who thinks of everything didn't think of this. "It's only a short drive. Didn't think I'd need one."

He brings the car to a stop outside a *Welcome to Doverfield* sign. It looks like a small village set within a natural decline. Almost all the lights are off, except a few pockets of yellow here and there.

"There's always a plan," he says, seeming to make a point of staring at me in the mirror. "Dad used to talk about You Know Who's plan all the time." He put emphasis on *you know who.* "If Mum had to take ten men up her tunnel in one night, well then, God was the tollbooth operator and it was all good." He smiles in what would be a handsome way if he wasn't a monster. Somehow, I know he'd be angry if I refused to meet the accusation in his glare. "Or was this Katy's plan, hmm?"

"What?" I say.

"Please don't insult me," he says. "Is this tyre a freak accident?"

"I g-g-guh…"

"Jesus Christ. Did you stutter as a kid or something? You sound retarded." I flinch on the last word, and he explodes in laughter. "Oh – here we go. You've been kidnapped. You've got no hope. You know I'm capable and, honestly, very willing to murder. But you still can't hide that oh-so civilised sensibility of yours. *Retarded.*" He chuckles again. "Retarded, retarded. Spastic." He claps his hands. "You're actually *wincing* every single time I say those words. Pathetic."

"Those are ugly words. If I'm reacting, it's for a reason."

He drums his fingers on the steering wheel. "If you allow words to affect you, you're nothing more than a sheep, a mark. Do you know how easy it is to manipulate somebody who places that much weight on words? I've won fights like that many, many times. A man wants to act tough, call his girlfriend a fat disgusting slut, just say the words, and his face goes red, his fists start to shake, his brain floods with adrenaline – he can't think. It's easy."

"I suppose you enjoy the power words give you," I tell him. "Because of your…" *Psychopathy.* "Thick skin, you're able to use words like weapons. I suppose it makes you feel very strong."

"Yes, yes – and not at all like the scared boy listening to his mother get piped in the next room. I know. Very good. Don't think I've forgotten about this tyre. You had the chance to puncture it."

"With what?" I snap.

"I don't know. A rock. A piece of glass. You're a resourceful person."

"If I had a piece of glass or a rock, I wouldn't be using it on a tyre."

"But you already tried running once. You know there's no point. You know I'll either hurt you or somebody else."

"I didn't do anything to the tyre," I snap.

"I'd ask you to swear on your husband – or your child – or even your pet, but you don't have any of those, Katy. You're a classic example of a sad, lonely modern woman. There's nothing in your life but isolation. You've been going to your sad little jujitsu classes for years and you still haven't got any real friends."

I try not to let his words sting, but the friend comment really hurts. I've sometimes felt like the odd one out, it's true. Mum says I always have my defences up. She says I was like that as a child, but it got worse after The Incident… the *rape*. Fuck it. It got far worse. And who can blame me, really? But even letting somebody get close emotionally feels like a violation of my body.

"Is that an example of using words as a weapon?" I ask. "Which is, by the way, not the revolutionary, mind-blowing concept you seem to believe it is. *Sticks and stones*… even children know that."

"Well done for not stuttering. Very impressive. Swear on your *mummy*, then, that you didn't do anything to the tyre."

"I swear," I tell him.

"It doesn't mean much," he replies. "You're not religious. Neither am I, strictly speaking, but I'm not arrogant enough to assume I understand what forces are at work. That swearing might mean more than you think."

"Then it's good I didn't touch it."

"You know what?" He's suddenly youthful and invigorated, rubbing his hands together. "I'm going to see this as an opportunity. I was going to drive to your next little surprise. But who knows what surprises this little village might have, hmm? I bet there's lots of interesting people to meet." He turns, pushing his face close to the divider. "I'm assuming I don't have to make any threats here, Katy. If you try to run or fight me, I'll seriously hurt you. But let's say you manage to get away, let's say you run into somebody's house – what then, do you imagine?"

"Nothing good."

"No, no. Be specific."

"You'll kill them."

"Yep… and lastly, if you manage to get away from me without escaping into somebody's home, I'll go into the closest house and murder everybody inside. Then, honestly, I might just go from house to house slaughtering people until the police find me. Do you understand?"

How the hell am I supposed to get out of this, then? My plan was to find a chance to get away. But unless he's bluffing – and I know he isn't – that would be like killing those people myself.

"Yes."

He claps his hands. "Good, then. Let's get going. Mission: find a car. Sub-objective: see what fun we can have on the way. Oh, and I've got an idea. But you have to play along."

23

MARTIN

There are plenty of spirals in the stars if a man knows the right place to look. A veritable conflagration of patterns unseeable to the eye of regular folk. I'm in the garden – at least, my bare feet are cool and the air is fresh – but I could be anywhere. Darkness surrounds me and I imagine I'm balancing on the back of a giant turtle surging across the ocean instead of being what I am: an old man with an ancient body and far too little to live for. Polly would call me morbid for that, but she can't call me anything now. She's dead, the love of my life, married forty-two years, in the dirt, being eaten by worms, slowly becoming atoms.

I lean on my walking stick, feeling it sink into the earth, hating the need for it. Shaggy yaps up at me, as he always does. He's a good enough dog, a bearded Jack Russell terrier, but I've never liked his name much. *Shaggy*. It was Polly's idea. I loved my dog more when my wife was alive. I wonder what that says about me. Maybe, more than anything, I loved her reactions to my treatment of Shaggy. Seeing me rub his chin let her see a gentle side of me. We never had children. All my family is dead. It's just me and Shaggy. He barks again.

I look down at him, shaking my head. His eyes are gleaming and the rest of his dark fur is hidden in the darkness. His fangs and his tongue flash with moisture. I remember years ago, maybe ten – it's deranged how quickly ten years transforms from an epoch to a hiccough – writing a story about a dog. I'm eighty-seven now, so that means when I turned seventy-seven I became a published author. I was a shopkeeper before that. A nice simple life with my wife.

No, that's not right. Polly *was* my life. That's one of the reasons I've taken to standing out here. I saw a documentary where a scientist said the dead become stars. Another reason is that I sometimes look over at the silhouette of our sturdy apple tree and think about hauling myself up on a ladder, taking a glorious bite of a glorious apple, and then tying a rope around my neck.

Shaggy barks again. I look down – another bark, from behind me. I turn… the process takes an absurd amount of time. I used to play rugby before my hip got a grudge against my hobby and wouldn't let me anymore. Shaggy is standing in the kitchen, the patio door closed. But he was out here. I saw him. No… I must've been *thinking* of him. Sound is a tricky thing. It can do unexpected things.

I limp over to the door, pull it open. He pitter-patters onto the cobblestones, nose down, sniffing. That's all he's been doing these past six months, sniffing for Polly. He must be able to scent traces of her in the grass. The garden's already becoming overgrown without Polly here to tend it. Walking into the kitchen, I see *her* again. Angela Starch, or as we used to call her, Angela *Tart*. A cruel nickname, perhaps, but it was one I was always happy to use back in the school days. She once asked me to the disco only to stand me up, just so her friends could laugh at me, make my life a misery.

Weeks ago – I think – she decided to continue her torture. She won't leave my house. She likes to smirk at me every time I mention it. I do my best to ignore her, keeping my eyes down. She often tries to tempt me by cooking chicken or wearing perfume of the tarty variety.

"Did you get lots of fresh air?"

What sort of question is that? I'm not even sure how to answer it. Perhaps she wants me to quantify down to the decimal. I remember it was after maths class when she and her friends walked by the boys' school, spotted me just minding my own business, and then they all pointed and laughed and made me feel so small. It took me a long time to even try to feel like a boy again after that. Girls don't know how much we care.

I sit in my chair near the electric fire. I'm wary of this because I know Angela might tamper with it to cause me harm, but it's the warmest place in here since the bitch won't turn the central heating on. And anyway, let me burn. Then maybe I can see Polly again. Shaggy sits at my feet, like he always does, nice and warm. Maybe he's an all right dog. I just wish I could stop thinking of Polly smiling at us every time I look at this little rascal.

Angela sits in the other chair. This was mine and Polly's favourite nook when she was cooking a meal. Now, the kitchen is scentless.

"Do you think you'll get much sleep tonight?"

"How the fuck would I know that?" I snap.

She does her *woe is me* flinch. It's like she's forgotten everything that's happened between us. Sometimes I wonder how long she's been here. She must've been waiting for the cancer to eat away at Polly, biding her time. It's psychotic. But the idea of escape exhausts me too much. She must be putting something in my food – a vicious cycle… She drugs me, makes me tired, I don't want to cook then, I eat her food, and on and on and on.

"I just meant… how do you feel, darling?"

"Don't call me darling, you vile bitch."

"Martin, please," she says, sounding like she might *cry* now. It has been tiresome since the first time she turned on the faucet, and yet she persists.

"If I wasn't old and broken I'd break you. Be quiet."

Finally, she gets up and leaves in a huff of sobbing and croaking and melodrama. Even Shaggy gets up and huffs and then leaves me. Fine, I'll just sit here, next to this heater, and I'll wait to die. I'll let her drug me. She's doing me a favour. Kill me so I can see my Polly again. We met in Brighton. I was showing off with some of my friends, most of whom are dead now, doing flips on the beach, trying to catch her eye, Polly with the blonde hair and the shy smile and the eyes that just drew a man in, in, in.

From the next room, I can just about hear Angela Tart on the phone. "He's not sleeping… and I just – oh, I don't know if I can do it anymore." A pause. "But it's not just about *me*. I have to think of him." Another pause. "How is that putting *him* first? If I'm going to contemplate this, I have to be honest. It's for me." Another pause. "Well… no, he'd hate it if he could see himself."

She's trying to twist people against me. I can't even think who she could be talking to. Maybe one of that gaggle of girls, each of them getting their digs in, silly skinny Martin with his hand-me-down shoes and awkward gait. I injured my ankle when I was a boy and it has hurt ever since, hence the walk. Is that a reason to make a child's life a misery?

Oh, and here she is, Angela Tart, with Shaggy walking just ahead of her. She sits down in an annoyingly dignified manner, as though she thinks she's the starring role in a Hollywood production. I loved Polly because everything she did and said was authentic. Angela is porcelain.

"Martin," she says. "I think we have to talk…"

"I'm fine just sitting here."

"About your care situation."

"My… care?" What new form of madness is this? "It's very simple. You feed and wash and poison me, and I resist the urge to kill you. I thought we had a fine setup. Surely I'll be dead soon, anyway? How strong is the poison? Do *not* cry!"

Suddenly, it's like I'm a young man again. This feels good. My right arm has de-aged six decades. I slam my fist down on the chair and sit up, my voice booming. I feel drunk with the suddenness of the change. "*I am sick and tired of these waterworks, you slut!*"

I don't even need the stick when I stand up. My hands are at my sides. I make my voice even louder as I beat my chest. A strike which should render me useless. But my strong fist bounces off my strong chest and I'm able to do it again. Angela Tart has retreated into the kitchen.

"Martin!" she wails.

Maybe this is the best way, not a slow poisoning, but a fight. Let her do her worst. She can even use a weapon. Nothing matters. If Polly was here – the stars are bleeding – the world is rushing… I stumble backward, dammit, fall into the chair. My head hurts. I keel over and vomit all over the floor.

"Oh, Martin." Suddenly, Angela Tart is approaching me again. She's got her hands in front of her. "Please, don't hurt me."

Another wave of sickness hits me. More vomit.

"I can't hurt anybody," I admit, painfully, both physically and for the soul.

I suffer the indignity of having Angela mop at my mouth and clean up my mess, and then she makes me drink a glass of water, no doubt with more poison in.

"What are you doing?" I snap, when she starts touching my arm.

"Checking if you've hurt yourself."

"Don't touch me, woman."

She cringes away. "Would it be so bad?" she asks from *behind* her chair now, standing. At least she has the sense to keep some distance between us.

"For you to touch me? Yes, you absolute moronic whore, it would. There's only one woman I want in my life. I'd die before I touched anybody else. Let me tell you something *your* slut soul would know nothing about. I lost my virginity to the woman I married and I never even looked at anybody else. Not *once*. Not even in my own mind. That's the type of love you know nothing about."

More tears. Jesus Christ. She's shaking all over, so much so that the chair she's clutching is juddering up and down, and the display is causing Shaggy to bark up at her. The disloyal mutt leaps onto the chair to try to lick the bitch. Maybe that's it: why he's betrayed Polly. A bitch and a dog go paw in paw.

"Oh, Martin," she wails. "I'm sorry – I can't do this anymore. I'm going to find you some care. Some *real* care. You're tearing my heart to pieces."

"I don't care about your heart." I want to shout, but my chest hurts. It must be a cold. Or something from the water. And my arm hurts. My whole body aches. How? I feel like I've had a tumble down the stairs. "There was one heart I cared about. It was bright and pure and only wanted to do good in the world. She thought I was going to leave her when she couldn't give me children. Worse than that, you tart, she said I *could*. She knew I wanted them. Do you know what I told her?"

Through her tears, Angela says, "You'd rather spend one year with just her than an entire life with a different family."

"How do you know that?" I demand.

"Oh, Martin…"

"*Oh, Martin*. Is that all you're capable of saying?"

Shaggy begins to bark before the doorbell rings. He rushes toward the front window.

"Visitors, at this hour?" Angela Tart says, walking toward the hallway.

24

HIM

There's this rushing, pulsing, interesting energy in my body and my mind. I've never done this before. The script has changed. This is, suddenly, as new for me as it is for Katy. She stands at my side, her hands wrapped across her middle, being docile and well behaved… for now.

This house is upscale, ivy creepers, sturdy stone build, a long, wide driveway separated by hedges. I only saw the lights on because of the angle of the terrain. Nobody in the adjacent houses would be able to see much of what happens on this property.

I peer through the vertical window next to the door as an elderly lady approaches. She's got a sinewy look, a toughness in her demeanour. I'm good at identifying weak people and she, although physically a non-factor, obviously, isn't weak.

"I hope you don't make me kill this woman," I tell Katy. "Two elderly ladies in one night might wear on my soul."

Mistake number one – the woman *opens the door*. The safeness of society has led to a massive decrease in basic awareness. Never, ever open your door to a stranger, preferably at any time, but definitely at night, and especially if you're old or female or otherwise less capable. I'm sure she feels a prickling discomfort at the sight of us, but she's ignoring it, letting her British sensibilities overrule her reason.

"I'm *so* sorry to bother you, miss." I've got my head bowed, behaving as her son might if he's done something wrong. It's a surefire way to make old women like me. "I know this must be very surprising and inconvenient for you. Believe me, I wouldn't be here if I had another option."

This disarms her. I've put myself at her feet. She's still slightly wary, but her posture has relaxed slightly. "It's no bother. I wasn't sleeping."

"It's a delicate matter. See, my sister here…" I nod at Katy, who's staring off into space like we agreed, looking spaced-out and weird. I lean forward, lowering my voice. "She suffers from schizophrenia. She's had us all worried sick tonight, driving all the way into the woods. She's been leading me on a wild goose chase. Anyway, long story short is, my car is broken – don't ask me how, I'm no mechanic…"

A charming smile, a chuckle, staring into her eyes, willing her to laugh. And she does. I haven't said anything funny. It's the middle of the night. I've just told her this woman is mentally ill. We're strangers. And she's laughing.

"And my mobile is out of battery. She took the train out here and she's ditched her mobile. I was wondering if…"

"The phone?" she says. "Of course."

I could probably gain entry here, but it's always better to put in the extra effort to obliterate their defences. Much of this – most of it, in fact – is non-verbal. It's in the subtle changes in my posture, the eye contact, the careful shape of my smile. Lots of people *think* they can fake emotion well, but they're transparent. I'm Oscar-worthy every time.

"Please," I tell her, gesturing at Katy. "I'll stay out here and use your mobile. I know this must be troubling for you. I don't want to distress you."

That's clever. She's a tough old root of a woman, probably thinks she's far more capable than she is. Who am I, she's thinking, telling *her* not to be distressed?

She leans in. "Is your sister…"

"She's not violent in the least," I tell her. "But I understand that people have certain opinions about the mentally ill…"

Here I am, a son-like figure, subtly challenging her empathy and, in a roundabout way, how up to date her politics are. Women tend to be far more accepting and modern than men. Even elderly women are like that, generally speaking. She tuts, shakes her head. "Poor thing must be freezing. Let's get you both *inside* where you can use the phone in the warm."

"Are you sure?" I put my hand on my chest.

"Please. I insist."

Katy looks up, just like I told her. Smiles, just how I said. *If our story works, when the moment comes, I want you to seal the deal*. "Thank you so much," she says.

The woman beams. She'll tell her friends about this, the chance she has to be nice to a madwoman. How progressive.

"It's no trouble at *all*, dear."

But it is. It's big trouble.

Katy gives me a look. I'm getting better at reading her. It's like I can peel off her skin, crack her forehead and drive my hand through the gooey matter of her brain, and pick at her thoughts. *Let's just get the car and leave*. That's the look.

I give her one right back. *We'll see.*

25

KATY

What am I supposed to do here other than go along with this deranged story? Markus became a different person when he was convincing the lady to let us in. It was so convincing, I almost started to believe him. It's a strange effect, *knowing* he's a monster but *feeling* like I want to trust him. The fact that it's all an act made no difference.

"We'll go in here," the lady says, gesturing into a living room.

Markus pauses, nodding down the hallway toward a closed door. Light shines through the clouded glass. "Is the pooch in there?" he asks. "I heard him barking."

"Yes, I had to shut him away. He's in there with my husband. My husband is… well, it's best if we go in here."

"Of course, miss… I'm sorry, what's your name, if you don't mind me asking?"

"Polly," she says, leading us into a quaint living room, one wall entirely taken up with photos of dogs. When she sees me looking, Polly says, "Those go back to the sixties. Lots of animals. Lots of memories. The phone is there…"

"Markus," he says. "And this is Katy."

"Would you like something to drink, Markus, Katy?"

"A cup of tea would work wonders," Markus says, so damn convincing. "Two cups. Katy might not drink hers, but if you don't mind…"

"Of course."

She leaves the room. Markus sits in the armchair and picks up the phone, a creepy-as-*fuck* grin slowly peeling across his face as he holds it to his ear. He starts talking loudly. "Yes, and the address is… Yes, the car just refuses to work. I understand it's very late."

Markus "hangs up" the phone and leans over to me, shaking his head in disbelief. When he speaks, it's in his regular voice, low and cutting and sarcastic. "This is absolutely obscene, the fact we're sitting here. This woman doesn't even seem mentally ill."

"You tricked her," I whisper.

"I told her you were a schizoid," he says, more to himself than to me. "And she let us in anyway. Maybe I'll make you stab her…"

"You're a good act—"

"Shut up," he says, and like an obedient pet, my mouth snaps shut. It's pathetic how quickly it happens. I've made this so much worse, bringing this here. He turns and lights up like a firework show when Polly walks through the door holding a tray of biscuits. "Oh, please…" He stands, hand on his heart again. If the prick has one. "You didn't have to go to all this effort. You're an angel."

I can't tell if he's flirting with her or appealing to her maternal nature. It seems almost a mixture of both, the way she flushes, like she wants to care for him. But she wouldn't mind if he kissed her, either. She averts her gaze, flushes, leans over as she puts the tray down.

From the next room, a dog barks again.

"Are you sure we can't say hello to the pup?" he asks, my skin crawling, my mind flashing with ugly images.

"He's better off with my husband," she replies.

"What about the man of the house?" Markus goes on, still on his feet, looking so huge and terrifying compared with her frail small body, but she doesn't realise it. She's probably thinking, *Oh, I wonder if he plays rugby...*

"He's… tired."

Markus takes a step back, way over the top. "I'm sorry. I've overstepped. I've got minor autistic traits, Polly. Sometimes I miss the obvious. And now I'm making a complete fool of myself and…"

"Oh, dear, no." She looks mortified. He's a slimeball. "It's nothing you've said. He's just going through a rough patch."

"Ah, the classic British reticence. *Rough patch* could be a light drizzle or a rainstorm. Thank you ever so much for the biscuits." He sits, and I watch as Polly tries to fit it into place. Markus has either slipped or he's getting bored, because that was abrupt, his sympathy melting as quickly as it froze into place. He looks up, then corrects himself, sits forward. "I'm trying to pretend I never put my foot in it, Polly." He winks, and then she thinks, *Oh, he's just a little strange. They both are. I'll do this nice thing for them and then they'll be on their way.* "Please allow me to save face."

She sits down, folds her hands, a dignified, pretty woman. "It's our ages, dear."

"We do rather bandy it about sometimes, do we not?"

Do we not. It's not just his voice that changes. It's everything, down to his mannerisms.

"I couldn't possibly comment," Polly says, with a youthful grin. "I'm just happy I don't have social media. Or even a bloody mobile!"

"You and your husband don't have mobile phones?" Markus asks.

"I can't tolerate them. And they can't tolerate me."

Markus laughs, and Polly flushes some more. I sit here thinking about the fact that her husband is clearly ill and vulnerable, and I can't tell them who this man is, because it'll all happen again. Blood, more blood – I have to stop it. I have to try. But how?

26

MARTIN

She thinks I can't hear them in there conspiring against me. I'm not sure what the plot is. But there's something dark about the mutterings coming from the place beyond the wall behind me. I'm sat on the chair in my kitchen with my dog at my feet. I'm sharp and clued-in, and I don't forget, and I don't forgive. That bitch has got someone in there with her, a man's charming voice – I wish he could charm her out of this house – and a young girl, it sounds like.

"Hmm, hmm, *hmm*, you've really outdone yourself with these biscuits."

"Opening the packet was the extent of my input, I'm afraid."

God, Angela Tart's voice is infuriating. She did that to me when she asked me to the dance: got all flirty, got me thinking she really liked me, lots of eyebrows and smiles and red cheeks and demure gestures poisoning my defenceless mind.

"Well, you deserve a gold medal," the man says.

Shaggy yaps up at me. I blink, close my eyes, open them, blink. He is smearing across the kitchen in a melting fire of colour, hundreds of them bleeding and ripping apart. Too damn watery, these old eyes. I lift my hand, rub at them, miss and hit my nose. Pathetic. And now I'm going to let them get me.

"Polly, may I say something?"

That was the really sick part. Angela Tart had given *his* wife's name to these schemers. Of course, she couldn't tell them the real reason for her being in their house. But sooner or later, they'll learn the truth. Even then, now, *was*, is… My head – *focus, little shit*… That's my dad and there's a belt in his hand. Suddenly, I'm back in the kitchen and Shaggy isn't bleeding anymore. He whines and rubs his beardy Jack Russell face against my leg.

Reaching down – my arms hurt terribly – I let him rub against my hand. There are tears in my eyes; that's why everything was bleeding. Time is moving so slowly, and I never knew sadness like this existed.

"Yes," Angela Tart finally, finally responds.

"I wouldn't presume to press you about your husband's business, but I like to think I can read people. Because of my minor autism, I've had to make a skill of it. I can see how sad you are. I just want to say… I know you're trying your hardest. You're doing a good job. You're a good person."

No, no, this isn't sadness. What a wimp I am to misbrand this gift. This is white-hot and Satanic and boiling right from the depths of a man, the place that's birthed when he stops being a boy, when he sees his father hit his mother or feels the fist himself. This is making me strong again. The pain ebbs away.

Suddenly, the door snaps open. I pretend to be the weakling they want me to be. Angela Tart sniffles and wipes at her nose, then grabs her knees and bends over and cries quietly just like Polly used to do. She blurs and the world rips apart and then something magical happens. Nothing else matters. Oh my Lord. Jesus, Mother and Joseph. This is a sight to behold. This is enough to make a man let every bad thought he's ever had go.

Maybe I've been dying all night, and I'm finally where I want to be.

It's Polly, my wife, my love for her burning so hot I can see the shape of her skeleton beneath her skin, can see her at every age from sixteen to eighty-seven. I can see every laugh and every sadness and every time she playfully poked me in the belly or giggled as I swept her into my arms. I can feel it all, and it infuses me more than any anger ever could.

"Polly," I whisper. "It's okay. Oh, love."

She gasps, rushes over to me. She's *right there*. My wife, the woman I thought I'd lost. I can't stop crying as I press my hands against her hips and feel the shape of her, the solidity. She's as real as my pain has been all these months. "Polly." I burst into tears and pull her against me. "Oh, Polly."

She wraps her arms around me, pushing her face against my chest as she did when she was alive. She's clutching on to me so tightly. She only ever really lets herself cry when I'm here to catch the tears. She pushes her face hard against my chest like she's been waiting for this moment. And so have I.

"I love you so much, dear," I tell her, and my silly petal looks up at me like she's surprised.

"I – I love you too."

I kiss her on the lips now. She makes me feel young and full of life. I don't need a stick to walk. I don't need the painkillers and I don't need any of your fancy yoga workouts, thank you very much. I just need my Polly!

She presses against my chest. I can tell she wants me to keep kissing her. I always knew. I could always tell if I was in for just a kiss or if there was a chance of something more. She wants to, but… "We've got company," she says.

She says, she says, she sells seashells on the seashore. There was a snake who ate the world, apparently. I remember reading about it in a book. I was sitting in a café window and the sea was crashing and then I looked down and Angela Tart was staring up at me with her hands on me, touching me, the sickness of it, the perversion. "Get away from me, you empty-headed whore."

Oh, and here they come. How predictable. The waterworks.

"Is everything all right in there?"

I turn, look down the hallway. It's one of – of them. That's it. Angela Tart and her conspiring maggots. At least Shaggy is on my side, standing in the hallway with his tail bravely perked, ready to fight for his human, his family. He growls, that deep one from low in his throat when there's a squirrel he wants to chase.

The man is tall, broad, a fit-looking man with eyes that make me wonder if I'm losing my noggin. Two different colours, noticeably so. I never really pay much attention to that sort of thing. He's wearing slightly dirty clothes.

I reach out for my stick, but I haven't got it. Where is my stick. And now the world is toppling sideways.

"Easy there, big fella."

Suddenly, the man has his broad arm around me. What chance do I stand against him? Give me forty years, fifty, but Christ, a man needs some help in this kind of situation. I need to play dumb until he gets those strong hands off me. Shaggy is just barking uselessly at me as the man cradles me against him like a Goliath who's found David lacking his slingshot.

"I'm sorry, sir," the man says. *Sir*. As if I'm going to fall for that. "I just don't want you to fall."

"I just need my stick," I tell him.

A quiet, strange-looking woman walks over to my chair and picks up my stick. She silently walks over to me, hands it to me.

"Thank you, sweetheart," I tell her.

"I'd be careful with such sexist language as that," the man says, laughing as he herds me toward my chair, pushes me really.

The impact of his forced speed on my knees isn't exactly pleasant. "*Sweetheart*. My sister's mental, sir."

"Stop calling me sir. I know what you're all up to."

"Martin…" Angela Tart thinks she can persuade me with that slippery, sick tone. The stupid bitch.

But she's right, though not for the reasons he thinks. I'm not being rude. But I am being incautious. They can't know what I'm going to do. *Ring, ring*. That's it. Just remember that. *Ring, ring*. If I can keep that sound lodged in my head, even if they try and distract me, I'm doing the right thing.

Ring, ring.

"She's a feminist, my sister," the man goes on, standing over me. He's probably the maverick of this little ragtag sabotage operation. "She once walked through London with her tits out to emphasise that men shouldn't stare at her tits. So don't call her *sweetheart*."

"It's—"

Something strange happens. When the young woman starts to speak, the man spins, turns demonic, and she closes her mouth like he has physically slammed it shut for her.

"Fine," she says a second later.

"Oh, it's fine," the man says, chuckling down at me. "Hear that, old timer? It's fine."

"How long until they're here, Markus?" Angela Tart, of course, has to pipe up and get involved.

"How long until who's here?" I ask, reasonably.

"The car service," the man apparently called Markus says. "Let me check." He takes out his phone, taps a few buttons. "I've got live tracking. He'll be here in twenty or so minutes."

Angela Tart pipes up. "I-I thought you didn't have your phone?"

"I meant phone *signal*. Look, Martin."

The man shoves the phone in my face. The bright screen shows a jumble of something, I don't know.

"Do you see it?" he asks, like he's the toughest cock in the pen.

"Of course I bloody do."

"It's better if we wait in the living room," Angela says. *The living room*. She speaks as if she has a right to it.

Shaggy finally remembers his duty. He growls and walks over to us, staring up at Markus.

"What a little rascal," the man says – Mark, Martian. The alien. What was his *name?* What sort of man comes into another man's home and doesn't give his name? "What's all that barking about, hmm? Are you going to bite me, you little demon?"

"It's really better if we wait elsewhere," Angela Tart says. Go on, Angela, you put that civilised quiver in your voice. You act like you wouldn't shout at *me* to wait elsewhere, you and your bitch friends, laughing from behind the fence.

"You're not going to hurt me," the man says, reaching out toward Shaggy.

Go on, Shaggy. Bite his fingers off and swallow them and then spit the blood in his face. But Shaggy has been in the warm for too long, just like me, letting myself get soft with Angela's poisonous tending hands. He stops growling, and then lets the man stroke him under the chin. The traitor.

"It's okay, boy," the man says, in a voice that somehow seems designed to calm both creature and person. "Oh, that's a good boy. Yes you are…"

It's not long before the man has scooped Shaggy into his arms. He grumbles a couple of times, but soon stops when the man cradles him like a baby and starts rubbing his belly.

"See?" He turns to Angela, as if her opinion matters. But I suppose it does when it comes to Shaggy. After this display, he's no longer my dog. "It's no bother. Your husband is safe and happy and, it seems, no longer assaulting you. And your little doggy just makes the best companion. Don't you, boy?"

"Martin was not…" Angela huffs. "*Please*, can we just return to the living room? Twenty minutes, you said? I'm ever so sorry. It's been a long evening."

27

HIM

Even now, with her pet in my arms, with the little signals I've let slip, she's trying to maintain some sense of control. I've overstepped her boundaries again and again. I'm in her home; she's asked me to leave a room several times. But I just stand here. People often respond in shock to these small violations. They've never experienced them before, and they're stunned at how complicated their problem becomes. If I were to, say, punch Martin, she would scream and panic and it would be clear. If I accidentally spilled something, she would *oh don't you bother yourself* at me. But these are too big to let pass and too small to riot over.

I hold the dog, let it lick at my cheek. I've got a high tolerance for disgust. It's impractical to have any sort of reflexive reaction when my passion brings me into contact with all kinds of matter.

"Twenty minutes, yes," I say, tickling her unfaithful hound on the scruff of its neck as I hold it with my other hand. I can feel its knobbly spine as I stroke it and it opens its mouth and drools.

"Right, then." She gestures toward the hallway, as if that's it. I can tell that took a *big* effort from her. This, to her, is rude. Becoming the tiniest bit stern with a stranger in her home in the middle of the night. She's a wreck. All people are. They sicken me. The indecision. The shameful disregard of intuition.

"Right, then," I echo, smiling over at her as I continue to hold her dog and stand within striking distance of her husband. Katy is leaning against the wall between us. She had her little protest. *It's fine*. Now, she knows to keep her mouth shut. She lied about the tyre – I'm sure of that – and now this.

"Shall we?" Polly says.

I could snap this indecisiveness in a heartbeat. *No, you bitch.* Watch her face change, the shock rippling across her wrinkles. But I walk the line. "I'm not sure. I'm quite enjoying *this* one's company."

"You can bring Shaggy." Oh, she's getting testy now. A little bite on that one.

"But you said he was keeping your husband company."

"He's a traitor," the old man grumbles. I can tell he would've been a problem had I arrived fifty years earlier, a tough, wide man with a large neck despite his age. If you want the measure of a man's strength, neck and legs, none of this gym-bro shit.

"I guess I'm keeping you, then, boy, huh?" It licks me some more. *Boy*. It's grotesque. I'm sure it would make a good enough pet, but *boy* is mentally deranged to a shocking degree, honestly. I turn, look down at the old oak. "Martin, with all due respect, please don't lay your hands on your wife."

"Please!" Polly almost downright erupts. I don't look at her.

The old man slowly turns to me, glares with watery eyes. I can see it in him, the young monster wanting to tear away all this old skin and be what he used to be, or a better version. Life is an ugly thing. By the time a man has the mental tools to make full use of his body, his body is already dying. But it seems this one's mind has too. It would be better to put him down. Let him jump off a cliff like the Vikings used to.

"Do I make myself clear?" I say.

Polly gasps. "Puh-please."

God, she sounds like Katy when she's stuttering. It's shameful, how much power she thinks she has with her words. Modern society has forgotten a very basic, simple fact: words are nothing without violence to back them up. In the olden days, a man said something, a man took a sword to the belly for it. A woman would keep her mouth mostly shut because she had no way to defend herself. I don't agree with all of that, obviously – women are far more interesting to me when allowed to roam alone – but the principle appeals to me.

"Martin?" I put Shaggy down, then kneel, looking up at the old man. "I don't want you hitting Polly when I'm here."

Polly sounds like she's on the verge of hyperventilating. Martin looks at me as if to say, *I see you. I know what you are.* He's watching me the same way a religious zealot would the devil. I play the part, offer him a well-constructed smirk.

Polly is now standing directly behind me. I can feel her, but I don't turn. It would be no effort at all to simply pivot from my kneeling position and slice the back of her knees with my arms. She'd fall, perhaps hit her head, but it doesn't matter. She'd fall and, being so brittle, become a non-entity in the fight. The dog would probably jump at me, so I'd take a few bites, perhaps, but only one of us would be able to carry on after a few violent motions. And then there's Katy and the man… No bother, honestly. Not exactly how I envisioned the night ending, but still.

"Markus," Polly says. "Please. I'll have to insist."

"My father beat my mother," I reply. "I'm sorry to share such shameful secrets about myself, but it's the truth. He beat her terribly. I can't stand for it."

"Martin would never hit me," she snaps. "You have no *clue* what you're talking about."

"Martin?" I say, grinning up at him, getting ready for it.

I can find another Katy, after all. She is immensely

interesting to me, especially with her assault and the whole self-defence angle. And, so far, she's been the most resilient. But it wouldn't matter *that* much. I like the researching stage anyway, the intimacy of getting to know somebody when they have no clue who I am. The thrill that comes with sleeping in the living room, waking a few minutes before her alarm, leaving the house.

Perhaps this is it, a chance to peak this evening. Whether or not Martin has ever laid a finger on Polly makes no difference to me.

"Martin?" Polly says desperately. "Will you tell him?"

"I never hit Polly, God rest her soul."

"God rest her soul?" I ask, smirking.

"Don't you grin at me, lad!" the old man booms. This is good. I can feel a trickle of adrenaline. This is going to be a night of epic proportions. I'm probably going to get caught, let's face it… If I stick around. Perhaps this is my last time in jolly old England. It's time I spread my wings and fly. A slaughter here and then a mad dash out of the country.

I grin wider.

He leans forward, looking strong and youthful, like his old self is pushing through his skin. That's good. I could do with a proper fight.

"Don't you smile about my dead wife!"

He moves far slower than me. Despite kneeling, I'm on my feet by the time he's dragged himself up. He squares up to me. The stupid dog starts barking senselessly.

"Please, both of you!" Polly whines, but then she starts to *scream*. "*Oh, Lord, dear girl! What have you done*?"

I turn quickly. Ah, clever. Katy is playing her part. She knows she can't warn these idiots. She knows she has no chance if she fights me.

She stands at the kitchen counter, a steak knife in her hand, dragging it across the back of her forearm – not her veins – over and over again. Blood weeps down her arm.

Remembering *my* role, I quickly rush over. There are several moments where she could lunge at me with the knife. I see her thinking about it as I reach for the handle. Then it's too late. I grip the handle hard, wondering. But this is interesting. That's real blood. It makes everything feel more significant.

"Do you have a first-aid kit?" I demand. "My sister is bleeding!"

"Oh, right, yes, of course."

Polly rushes from the room. I grab the bleeding arm, twist my hand around so I'm gripping the cuts. She begins to whine until I lean in and whisper, "Make a single noise and I'll break it."

She somehow stands there stoically as I squeeze harder and harder, making sure to rub my palm across the cuts. She takes every second of it.

Polly rushes into the room, her footsteps tap-tap-tapping against the kitchen floor. "Is she all right?"

The melodrama is ridiculous. These cuts are enough to make her bleed, but shallow enough not to be a real problem. They've already started to clot and stop bleeding.

"She'll be fine," I say, wiping my hand on her shirt front, feeling the shape of her breasts, before I turn around. "Let me tend to her and we'll join you in the living room."

"Shouldn't we call an ambulance?"

For a few scratches? "If I did that every time she pulled a stunt like this, we'd put the NHS out of business. And, Polly – Martin, I'm ever so sorry for delving into your personal business."

"Never mind that now," Polly says, but I can tell she's grateful. The stupid, blind cow.

28

MARTIN

"Are you sure we shouldn't call an ambulance?"

The merry band is sat around the kitchen table, the small one around which me and Polly used to sit and look into the garden, at all our dogs running together. Not together. But they do now, when I think about it, every hound we ever owned. And who owned us.

"She's fine, aren't you, Katy?"

At the table, a small voice, sounding almost feral. "Yes."

She's the attack dog of the pack, not Shaggy. She did something to her arm, made it red, made it weep, but I didn't see it all. I keep slipping. I wish they would leave. *Ring, ring.* What is that noise – *Ring, ring.* No, that's it. I remember now. They need to leave.

"I'd rather be alone," I say.

That's normally enough to get Angela huffing and moving away, but nobody at the table moves.

"Are you sure?" she asks.

"Won't you be lonely, Martin?" *he* asks, the devil-eyed son of a bitch. There's red in him. It's like the blood from the feral thing's arm is in his eyes. He's the mastermind behind this, whatever they've got planned for me. They're probably working up to it now, measuring their moment.

"I prefer to be alone these days," I tell the man. Martin – is that his name? It began with an *M*, I'm sure. Mar… Mars, red, blood-red. Wait. No. I'm in a hole. Falling. This isn't right. What's my name? Is that what these people are doing? This has to be a joke. I know my own name.

Ring, ring.

"Ring, ring?" Angela asks.

What is happening… How did she hear that? I stiffen my upper lip, don't let them see. They're probably waiting to see that this, whatever it is, is having its desired effect on me. But there's only so much a man can take. Put me in a field. Give me a gun. Anything but this.

"Your husband was in the army?" the man says…

And now they're all standing. Angela Tart is the closest. The man is facing the wall and the feral freak is standing with her bandaged arm across her belly. They've stolen my name and now they're stealing time from me too.

"I – uh, it's complicated."

"I just assumed from this photo…"

"I should take it down really."

"He looks handsome. Cutting."

"Yes," Angela Tart says. "He certainly does."

I don't listen to anything they're saying. I was a shopkeeper and that's all I ever needed to be. Angela Tart has said this sort of nonsense before, I'm almost sure of it. A humble shopkeeper would never be good enough for her. She needed to make everything more significant than it really was. Reality was enough for me and Polly.

"That sort of training never leaves a man," Martin says. I think that's his name. Martin. "It stays in his bones."

"Are you sure you want to be alone, dear?"

I say nothing, stare, hiding my reaction. Finally, they leave me. Shaggy walks at the man's feet like he's found his new owner. I don't let them see a single goddamn thing. I'd rather burrow my way to Hell and throw myself onto a pitchfork than let another man know he's had an effect on me. Let them cook up their spells in the living room.

Ring, ring. I look up at the phone on the wall. There's something significant about it. It sits there like it's hiding a secret my damned head won't let me puzzle out. There's something – I know what it does, obviously. A telephone allows people to communicate vocally. But there's something else, *who*. Maybe there's a…

Hands buried in my throat – blood and metal in my nostrils – getting my hand around the blade and…

I blink, stare at the phone, the red phone. It's green, vivid like a field, like skipping ahead of my mother and hearing her laugh and wishing my father was dead. *Ring, ring*. Why is this so difficult. Why is life so misshaped. Why are people so cruel. I'd rather a man punch me in the face than be left wondering if somebody is *going* to hurt me.

"Ring, ring," I whisper, licking my lips, moister than I expected. There's a glass of water on my side table. Did I pour it?

"It's a terrible thing," the man says through the walls, speaking loudly as if he wants me to hear. "Losing one's mind like that."

"I don't like to think of him as him *losing* it." Angela Tart is using her stern tone. Maybe she's having second thoughts about including these people. "He's there… just buried. Harder to find."

"I truly am sorry for imposing. I let my personal issues get in the way. I think I triggered Katy."

"Poor thing," Angela says.

"It's my autism." *Ring, ring.* "It really is a problem."

29

KATY

My arm pulses from the cuts… and from where Markus grabbed it. It was the only thing I could do. I didn't let myself think: just grabbed the knife, slid it, feeling my skin tear like wet paper. At least I avoided my veins. But it's produced an evil effect in Markus. He seems upbeat, like a man who, after a long week at work, is finally able to indulge in his hobby.

"You see, my *autism*," he says, glancing at me every time he uses that word. I know he's trying to bait me with his words-have-power schtick. As if I care about political sensibilities right now. I just want to stop this lady and her dog and her husband from – I can't even think it. "It makes me blind to certain things sometimes."

Polly is clearly running out of patience, tapping her foot, constantly glancing at the door. "Yes, well, it's no bother. How long does your phone thingy-ma-bob say your service will be?"

"Not long now," Markus says smoothly. "Would you like us to wait outside?"

I wonder what would happen if she said *yes*. She pauses, as if considering it. A strange combination of civility and sunk cost fallacy is working on her. She's invested all this time already. If she goes just a little further, she can still view this through her civilised lens. She was still the Good Samaritan. But Markus won't stop.

"Oh, no, it's just rather late."

"Come on, Katy…" Markus motions toward me.

"No, please," Polly says. "I insist."

Why? Markus sits back. "I truly am sorry to take advantage of your hospitality for so long. If it's any consolation, Katy likes you."

Polly frowns at me. I make myself smile, and I can tell it actually means a lot to her. She's clearly a kind woman. He's warping that.

"Don't you, Katy?" Markus says.

"Yes."

"But," Markus goes on, "I shouldn't really ask her that. Katy has got herself into trouble with saying *yes* before. When she gets certain episodes, she says *yes* to everything. I won't tell you how badly that ended."

Markus licks his lips with, somehow, an edge of violence. "Well – let's just say, one of the rugby lads asked her if she wanted to come to the changing rooms for a *party*." Markus leans forward, pinning Polly in place with his gaze. "I don't have to tell you what that means."

"How awful," Polly whispers.

"The thing is, Polly, Katy *enjoyed* it."

Polly's face begins to pale. This is so far outside of what she would consider acceptable conversation. That's what people like Markus do, even the lesser versions, the everyday manipulators. They push and push and push. It's probably amusing to him, the fact she's still letting us sit in her home. I bet it's exciting in a way he wouldn't even be able to describe. In his petty world, he's playing God.

"She was quiet at first, but, apparently, she started screaming for more."

"Oh, poor dear."

"Poor *dear*?" Markus says, laughing in a mean, aggressive way that tells me, soon, he's going to rip away the mask completely. He's got a new vicious edge. "By the end of it, she was screaming at them, demanding that they keep going. She was absolutely covered in—"

"Please. This is my home. I won't hear such talk."

"There she is, finally," Markus says, grinning. "I knew you had a bit of fire in you, Polly."

"Doesn't it seem rather ghastly to you, talking about your sister in that way?"

"It's difficult to respect a woman who'd do something like that, though," Markus says.

"She was a girl. Probably scared. Probably confused. I think it's a rather nasty thing to say, especially in front of her."

"Relax, cunt."

Markus grins. I almost gasp, then think better of it. Any second, he could snap. Polly doesn't even know how to register this. She just stares at him as if he's spoken a foreign language. She's probably never been called that word before, or at least not in years.

"Excuse me?" she says.

"I said… relax, cunt." Markus laughs, shaking his head. "Really, Polly, you're not a very intelligent woman."

She's on her feet fast, gesturing at the door. I can imagine her like this in a restaurant, a picture of outrage, demanding to speak to the person in charge. She thinks this show of fierceness will help her. But it won't. I'll have to act. I should've taken my chance to stab him. But would that have *stopped* him instantly? This night is teaching me a lot about real violence.

"I'd much rather you wait outside now, thank you very much!"

"I'm sure you would," Markus says. "But I quite like it in here."

"How long until—"

"Polly, please, use your head. You knew something was wrong the moment you opened the door. I saw it register on your face. That was your instinct. Female intuition… I happen to believe that's a real, reliable thing. Look at police reports – often, the women knew something was wrong, but they ignored their instincts. You're too kind. Too concerned with appearing rude or being embarrassed. It makes you extremely manipulatable."

She just stares, awestruck at the change in him. He's speaking in the way he speaks to me. Even his accent has subtly changed, become slightly rougher.

"What do you want?" Polly whispers.

"I'd like for you to sit down. I need time to think, make a decision."

"We need a car," I say.

Markus glares at me. "I haven't decided that yet."

"I've got a car. You can have it." Polly trembles as she sits down. "Please, just don't—"

"Nah-uh-uh," Markus says, tutting. "Don't become useless to me. I don't want any melodramatics. I'm interested to see where we can take this experience. But if you start crying and panicking and become so depressingly ordinary, what choice do I have, Polly?"

"Do you want money? I have jewellery. It was my mother's."

"I don't need much money," he tells her. "I may take a few items, though, thank you. Honestly, in this moment – taking this mad night as it comes – I'm more interested in stripping away your civilised veil. I know… Strip, Polly."

"Markus," I snap.

He turns to me, completely calm. "Interrupt again and I'll make you watch me bleed her dry. This isn't sexual." As though that justifies it. "I want to see her stripped bare. Her spirit and her body." He turns back to Polly. "Well? Chop, chop."

The lady has changed completely. It's like she's woken with her head in a bear trap. "Pluh—"

"No pleading. No reasoning. No chance. You either strip or I slaughter everybody in this house. I don't care *that* much."

Pathetically, I'm almost grateful he's forbidden me from speaking. It means I don't have to try and think of something I could possibly, possibly say. How am I supposed to make this better for her? I could attack him, maybe *should*. But will I win? No, no, I won't.

"Markus," she says.

"That's not my name, sweetheart," he replies, laughing. "She *is* called Katy, though. But she's not my sister. It's a long, red story. Don't you trouble your little civilised head about it. Just get on those achy feet of yours and show me your naked wrinkled flesh."

We all turn when bright headlights suddenly gleam onto the front window, shining through the curtain. There's the sound of an engine dying, a door whining open. Markus glares at me, then shakes his head, as if to himself. Then he looks at Polly. "Who is that, woman?"

"I don't know," Polly says, with a pleading tone. She's begging for her life. "I swear. I have no idea."

Footsteps walk audibly up the gravel, or maybe that's just my mind twisting itself into ugly, taunting hope. I can't let myself think there's a way out of this. Markus will kill us all.

"Do you usually get visitors this late?" Markus asks.

"No… tonight has been most unusual."

"*Most unusual*," Markus snaps, mimicking her upper-class tone.

Then – it's so sudden. I wonder if I blacked out for a moment. He has pushed her against the wall. He hits her in the gut and she lets out a breath that sounds like cracking ribs. "Let me tell you how this is going to go."

30

MARTIN

The doorbell rings. *Ring, ring.* I close my eyes tight and use my sharp, intelligent mind to try and remember how the doorbell is ringing already. I'm falling down a vertical corridor with exits on all sides, but I lack the athleticism to seize them, to leap with everything I have, to land and roll and safely disarm time. This damned thing. Twisting backwards and forwards.

"Act natural," the man is saying. He's turned on Angela Tart, it seems. That's fine with me. As long as I can get out of here, or get them killed, maybe die in the process, be with Polly. "Do you understand?"

"Yes," Angela Tart replies, affecting to make herself sound as afraid as possible.

Falling – hitting, now I'm on my feet, leaning against the counter as I dial the number. As I *dialled* the number. Angela and her ilk want to convince me I'm mad, but a madman wouldn't be able to accurately recall his old friend's phone number. And he wouldn't know that it had already happened, as soon as Angela had left the kitchen. I'm sure that's right.

On my feet, dialling the number, getting it wrong… a few times. But then the phone rang and his angry voice answered. He was – a good friend, a policeman, a retired policeman. We used to play rugby together. His name is, is he's a good friend, a retired policeman.

"Hello?" he snapped. "Do you know what time it is?"

"Be quiet," I told him. "I need you to listen."

"Martin?"

"They think they've already got me. But I remember those days. I remember when I left the forwards and joined the line, and you shook your head at me, but then I punched right through. We did it four more times that match. Remember?"

"Bloody hell. I haven't thought about that in years."

"And all those cheeky pints at the pub. You'd always adjust your coaster so it aligned with the table. It was the police officer in you. Everything in its place."

"What's this about, Martin?"

Martin. The word doesn't feel connected to me, but I'm sure my old friend kept calling me it.

"They're here," I told him. "They're making their final push."

"Who is?"

"Angela Tart and her friends."

"Angela, oh, Martin… what friends?"

"What friends?" I snapped. "Her conspirators. They're in there cooking something up!"

"Hang on. Let me get this straight. Are you saying there are people in your house?"

"Do I need to send you a photo? Isn't my word good enough?"

"It's not that, fella, just… Can I speak to Pol-ah, Angela, please?"

"Why would you need to speak with her?" I said, thinking about the fact he'd called me Martin. They were trying to trap me with that. It's all names are, I'm realising. They're not required. Reality just *is*. "Don't tell me you've forgotten those rugby days."

"Please let me speak with her."

"They're here. Two of them. There's already been blood. I saw it. Lots of blood—"

"Blood?"

"If you're any sort of man at all, you'll get here. Now. Or I'll just let them have me."

That's it… then I put the receiver down and returned to this chair, and now the doorbell is ringing again. *Ring, ring.* I'm not sure he's going to be able to stop them from completing their plan, whatever it is, but maybe that's not the point. Maybe this was always going to end in slaughter and pain. Maybe my job is to let that happen. So I can be with my wife.

More noise, a door opening. Angela Tart is all bright-voiced. Everything travels in this house. Noise. Fear. Resentment. "Charley?" Angela Tart says. "Isn't it a little late for a visit?"

"I'm so sorry, Polly."

Polly. Angela has somehow tricked him… or he's in on it too? How could she make him believe she was Polly?

"Martin rang. He sounded in a right bother. He said you had visitors."

"Oh – we do."

"At… half past one? It's the middle of the night."

"Poor things. Their car broke down. The girl, between us…" Her voice lowers. Classic Tart and her gossiping, secretive ways. "I'm sorry you wasted your time. But we're fine. You know what he's like these days."

There she goes, slagging me off. She doesn't know I can hear so much from this spot in the kitchen. It's as though it was designed for me, as if the architect of the house knew I'd one day have to suffer the indignity of being my childhood bully's plaything.

"Right, then," my old rugby friend says. "I guess I better be off. Thought I'd better check. But before I go, can I say hello to the old fella?"

"It's been quite a night for him…"

"But he remembered a lot on the phone. I'd like to shake his hand at least. He asked to see me."

"I don't know…"

"It won't take two ticks."

Footsteps in the hallway. The kitchen door opens. A big tree of a man walks in and kneels, then looks at me eye-to-eye. His old skin slides away and a young man stares at me with tape on his face and a rugby shirt on, trees blowing in the wind behind him.

"You all right, mush?" he says.

I look over at Angela. "Let me speak with my old friend alone."

Angela gets all scare-eyed and glances back down the hallway. She's probably wondering if her friends are going to be angry at her for not finishing the job. They've already made me forget my own name with their magic, their bullshit.

"I'm not sure that's a good idea," she finally says.

"Won't be two ticks," my friend says, a good man, getting to his feet and basically herding her from the room like the cow she is. He returns to me, lowers his voice. "What's all this about? You said there'd been *blood*?"

"The feral girl cut her arm. I think she's the attacker of the group, the beast, like a honey badger, all knives and nails and teeth. The man is the one in charge. I think maybe Angela hired him first, but now he's getting notions of power."

"Wait, slow down," he says, like he doesn't think I can punch through the line. "What do you mean, notions of power?"

"He's turned on her. But it doesn't matter. Their little squabble is about who leads their not-so-merry band. But their objective is the same. You have to stop them. Or get me away from them. Please."

"Is everything all right in here?" *he* says, the devil-eyed man. He's standing in the doorway, filling it up as though making a statement with his size. He truly is an impressively built person, just what you'd want for a hit like this.

"I'm just speaking with my friend," my old rugby pal says. I appreciate the effort, but I wish his voice hadn't trembled a bit at the end there. He corrects it a moment later. He ought to. He was a… *Damn it.* A fireman. He's used to pressure. "How long until your car service is here?"

"It's been delayed. Another twenty minutes. Sod's Law."

"And you don't have a mobile?"

"It's a long story. My sister is going through a rough time."

"Right," he murmurs.

The man does his peeling, weird smile. Maybe he thinks it's charming. It would probably work on weak people like Angela Tart and treacherous animals like Shaggy, but not on me. "*Right*? I can show you the app if you like. The car's on its way."

"How about this, then?" my friend says. "I'll give you two a ride to your vehicle. Saves you walking back up to it when that app tells you your man is there. I assume that's where he's heading – your car? Or is he picking you up here?"

"I think that's the VIP package," the man says, all smiley, but my friend isn't falling for it. He's a big tree of a human and this sort of nonsense can't penetrate his bark. "We'll be walking up to the car."

"All right then, that's sorted. I'll drive you up there. Let these folks get some rest."

"Hmm, no."

"No?" my friend says, like he can't fathom how somebody could refuse to see the logic in this. But that's the problem. He's thinking of this in a logical way. He doesn't understand that these people don't care about that. They exist in a different space, their objectives entirely twisted toward me.

"With all due respect, sir, I'd much prefer to wait in the warm. My sister is ill—"

"Then, with all due respect, she shouldn't be here. The last thing these folks need is to catch—"

"My mistake," the man cuts in, some of the devil in him showing when my friend continues to try and claim a piece of the conversation. "Her ailment isn't physical. It would cause her unnecessary distress to move her now."

"So it would be better to walk in the cold and the dark? Rather than drive?" My friend laughs gruffly, and I know it's a mistake. It's his policeman's laugh, his *are you having a laugh* laugh. It usually disarms people and makes them understand how silly they're being, but I can't imagine that working on Devil Eyes.

"Maybe you could wait with us," he says. "Kill two birds with one stone."

31

HIM

Our new guest takes a wide stance, his shoulders back. One foot is slightly behind the other. It seems instinctual, so he knows how to fight, or did, once. It never leaves a man's bones if he's done it enough times. He's old, but not infirm like Martin. Seventy or eighty years of sinew, his bushy grey eyebrows flaring to an almost comical degree. Hasn't this idiot ever heard of a nose trimmer? I wonder if Polly said anything to him at the door. I threatened her enough.

If she did, he was an idiot for coming in here. He should've got into his car and rang the police. No, she must not have said anything. It's the imbecile ancient with his delusions, most likely. I glance behind me, making sure Katy and Polly are still in view.

"It's a little late for that," the man says. "My wife will be worried."

"But you said you'd wait with us at the car anyway?" I ask, then I laugh, but it's getting more and more difficult to keep this mask on. It would be so much easier to just let myself blackout, wake up in a bloodbath as I have a few times before. But then I don't even remember it, can't mine anything from the experience.

Fine, then I could consciously kill them all. I'm not sure I want to do that yet.

"You've caught me," he says, holding his hands up, still civilised, but less than Polly and Martin. This one's got some bite in him. I'd bet he was in the armed forces, or maybe a boxer, a policeman perhaps. "I'm using an excuse because I want to give these folks some peace."

"I suppose I'm disturbing the peace, then?" I reply, still smiling, but letting him know nonverbally that I could tear his face off and force him to eat it if I wanted to. "Is that it…"

"Charles," the man says. "And you are?"

"Markus. It's a real pleasure."

He gestures to me, at the hallway behind me really. "Shall we?"

"I'm sorry to repeat myself. I thought I made it clear we'll be waiting here."

"I'm sorry too, Markus, but that isn't your choice to make."

I almost grind my teeth. *Almost*. But I catch myself at the last second. He's seriously got a deluded idea of who he is in his head. There's this look in those old eyes of his, surrounded by wrinkles. *Now I'm here, nobody has to worry*. He's used to being the man who solves all problems, like the moron who once fell in love with my mum. One of her customers. Dad found out and told her God had sent the man to make us richer, and so, together, they scammed him. Worked him over. Drained every penny.

"We'll be staying here," I tell him.

He glances behind me – I turn. Polly is standing within view. She looks at me wide-eyed and shocked. Was she just mouthing something? Gesturing? What was she doing? I want to grab her brittle wrist and wrench upward in a sudden, cruel motion, snapping her flimsy bone. Beyond her, Katy just stares.

Turning back, I find Charles watching me with a frown. "If you're staying, I'll wait with you. Drive you and your sister down to your car. No need to walk then. Kill two birds with one stone, like you said."

What could she have done to affect this change in his demeanour? Maybe she waved her hands, pleading. Or drew one finger across her throat to indicate murder. Whatever it is, I almost thank her. We're back to the game. Sooner or later, this ice will crack. And maybe oh-so reliable Charles thinks he'll drown me. But that's never how this ends. People have fought me before, many times. I'm stronger and faster and far more violent. People think they understand fighting until you chew off a piece of their face and spit in their eyes to blind them.

I grin. "Fantastic. I'm glad we're in agreement. Let's bring old Martin in with us. The more the merrier."

This is the truly telling moment. I see it register on Charles' face. He knows that, if we're truly existing in the civilised world still, then he has every right to say his friend would prefer to stay here. But he gets a hostage-like look, and it tells me everything I need to know. Polly gestured somehow. Charles knows the score. That means we all have to be in the same room. All the alive people, anyway. Dead men and tales and all that.

"What'd you think, old boy? Fancy a cuppa and a biscuit with your old friend?"

"You too," Martin says, sounding like he might cry. "I scored three times that game but every try was yours. And now you're all tarted up."

"He doesn't know what he's saying." Polly rushes past me. "Come on, Martin. We're all going to have a nice sit-down in the living room."

I walk down the hallway, grabbing Katy's wrist and holding her as Polly helps Martin through the door. Charles follows, looking just like Katy did earlier with the knife. He's contemplating all the things he could do, assessing, realising my youth and my calm gives me too much of an advantage. So he'll assure himself: *later, soon*... But later won't make a difference. And soon he'll be dead.

When he's inside, I lean close to Katy's ear. "What did Polly do?"

"What?"

"You heard me." I give her arm a shake, rattling her fragile frame. "Behind me. She did something. Gave a signal."

"I didn't see anything," Katy says.

That's twice she's lied to me. First about the tyre, now about this. "Okay, Katy. Whatever you say."

32

KATY

I think he knows I lied to him. I saw Polly waving her hands at Charles. I couldn't see her face, but I'm sure it said everything. Charles changed after that. We're all playing a role in Markus' personal play. The only one not aware is Martin, obviously, but I'm sure Charles is in on it. Pretending for Markus' sake. Perhaps he senses that, the second this performance stops, it's back to the gore and the horror.

"What happened to your arm, dear?" Charles says, sitting beside Martin on the sofa.

Without outright ordering them to, Markus has somehow arranged them at the furthest point from the door. He stands behind my chair, meaning he could intercept anybody trying to flee. "My sister doesn't speak much. She's mentally deranged, a proper freak. She once got so obsessed with martial arts she tried to karate chop her rapist. Can you believe that?"

They all gasp, but Markus gleefully goes on. I try not to let his words wound me, remembering what he said. None of this means anything to him. Words are just a tool to cause pain. He doesn't base anything from how he actually feels, because he has no feelings. My earlier plan of trying to therapise him was clearly madness. There's no way I can crack that demented head. I need to think about practicalities now, like what the four of us can do if we all move against him. But we won't all act in a quick, coordinated way. And even in the best-case scenario – if we all jumped on him at once – he could still somehow win.

"How awful," Charles says, shaking his head in that civilised way. He's still trying to play along, but he's letting little glimpses of panic through.

"What was your profession, Charles?"

The older man tries to laugh, but it sounds so forced, painful. "You assume I'm retired, do you?"

"I'm sorry. How rude of me… But am I wrong?"

"I was a police officer," Charles says with pride.

Without turning, I somehow know Markus' face has changed. I can feel the anger bursting from him like countless promises of violence. "Ah," he says. "How interesting. An upholder of this noble law of ours. Still, a country policeman. You couldn't have seen much action."

"In fact, I spent the majority of my career with the Met. I came here for a change of pace. Many years ago now."

"Many years ago? How many, exactly?"

"Six."

"So you've been retired for so many years, you've forgotten half of what you knew. Your body isn't what it used to be."

"I'm as fit as I've ever been," Charles says.

"No, my friend. I'm sorry – but no. An average twenty-five-year-old man would crack your elderly head on his fist and send you to the emergency room. Nobody can outrun Father Time."

Charles stands slowly. Shaggy walks around the coffee table, lies at Martin's feet. The old man grumbles and shoos the dog away. Charles looks down, then at me, then at Markus as though it costs him a great effort. He makes a point of staring at Markus for a few moments.

"I think it's time we stopped playing games, son."

"Sit down." Markus takes a menacing step forward. He's beside me, radiating violence. I could grab his sleeve, maybe, drag him down, try to get my arms around his throat. But it all feels so ineffectual now.

"Why don't you explain what's happening here," Charles says.

Markus doesn't say anything else. He just stands there with his fists clenched staring at the older man. Charles seems to weigh it up, then sits slowly, gripping his knees and looking up at Markus.

"A police officer used to fuck my mother," Markus goes on conversationally, then chuckles when Polly makes a sour expression. "Even now, Polly, you little tattletale, even *now* you've got that gloriously upstanding reaction to the true reality of this world. These bricks, this carpet, the walls, the windows, the central heating, strip it all away, but you've never felt it." He's sermonising, waving his hand. "This police officer would arrive via the back entrance and pay extra. My father had a good scheme going, got photos of the man, blackmailed him. He *bragged* about it right after our morning's prayer."

"Is this a robbery?" Charles snaps.

"You're determined to ruin the fun, aren't you?" Markus gives a proper woe-is-me sigh. "I'd like to talk about your police career, your personal life, a great many things. But you want to get right to the point."

"No point dragging this out, lad," Charles says, afraid but somehow meeting Markus' gaze. "Something's happening here. We both know it."

Idiot, I almost yell. But I can't speak. He's cut out my tongue. Playing this game was the only way to try to make this work.

I spring to my feet, start moaning, run to the display unit and slam my fist against it. I growl like a wildcat and do it again, feeling just like I did when that piece of filth grabbed me, dragged me into the dirt, laughed when I tried to defend myself. I scream and keep hitting, hissing, the taste and texture of gravelly dirt in my mouth and throat, and the stain of his kisses.

"Katy, Katy." His hands are on my shoulders, almost comforting… I cringe away from him.

He narrows his eyes, looking at me curiously, as if he's trying to work out if this is a trick. Even I don't know. My hand feels like it's beginning to swell and my knuckles are pulsing. Tears blur everything. Charles should do something now, *now*. But they just sit there.

"The performance is over," Markus says. "You're hurting yourself for no reason."

"I was *raped*." I walk right up to him, grab the front of his shirt, pull myself close so he can see right into my eyes. "All right? Is th-that what you want to hear? He *raped* me. He pinned me down and shoved dirt into my mouth and forced his erect penis into me against my will. *Okay*?" I'm screaming now. "I'll say it a thousand times! Just leave these people alone, please!"

33

MARTIN

The whole world and its mother can go to hell. There's nothing else for it. Shaggy is trying to make friends with me, but it's already over. Devil Eyes is blazing from the inside as he looks down at the feral girl, her fist swollen and purple, blood leaking from her eyes. I'm sitting atop the abyss, ready to fall when they make me, make me forget my name, and now I'll forget me. Everything. And maybe then I'll be with her. But Polly won't be where these people send me. Wherever she went, there was always light. There's going to be nothing but dark in my prison.

"I'm proud of you," Devil Eyes says, because of course he is. He probably found her in some swamp somewhere, a feral creature, trained her to act and look somewhat human. And finally, this explains how Angela Tart can appear as Polly to my, my police officer friend. It's their magic. "I know that must've been difficult to say."

"Can we just get a car and leave?"

"You want to go with me?"

Feral Girl puts her hand on Devil Eyes' shirt, almost lovingly. That's something I hadn't considered before – I think. Maybe they're lovers too. Perhaps she throws that small erratic body against his, and he grabs her, owns her, and she likes it even if she knows she shouldn't. I get a sinful feeling from them, somehow decadent. I hope this twisted ceremony doesn't take *that* turn.

"Of course I do."

"To save these people."

"Now hang on…" But one look from Devil Eyes has my old friend wilting. He shuts up and lets Satan go on.

"That's the only reason you want to come with me," the red burning creature says.

"No, that's a lie," the feral girl replies, sounding so passionate, so full of love, I'm almost jealous of the man, for a moment. "I've changed more in this one night than my entire life. You've shown me things… not just about others, but myself."

"Do you think I'm naïve, Katy?"

"It's the truth. I wish it wasn't, but it is. If it wasn't for you, I would've been calling my rape 'the incident' for the rest of my life."

"And I'm sure you would've been perfectly fine with that."

"You've shown me what I'm capable of, shown me my limits, shown me *myself*."

"Yes, a lovely speech—"

Bad idea. She slams her fist against his chest. "If you don't believe me, just do it, Markus! Just do it. But it's true. I want to go with you to see how you can keep helping me."

"You're telling me what I want to hear," Devil Eyes says, surprising me. He seems more amused than angry that she hit him. "But, do you know what, honestly, I *am* impressed. And there's no reason for more blood. It can get rather repetitive."

"So we can go?"

Yes, we're going, Shaggy says, putting his words into my mind. He's never spoken to me before – I think – like this or in any way. But it doesn't feel surprising. *They're going to copulate and then swallow us up like a wolf. I hope you're ready, old man. Thank you for all the treats and for always treating me with respect.*

"Fine, fine." Devil Eyes laughs. "Polly, be a dear and give me your car keys."

"Now hang on," my old friend says.

"Okay, Charles… I'm hanging."

"We can't just let you go." He stands up, and suddenly it's like the rugby, like when he'd stand at the middle of the scrum and give me a look like, *It's time to get them, lad, time to mess them up good.* My muscles tremble as I watch him walk toward Devil Eyes, not fearing the flames. "By the sounds of it, you've done bad things."

"How clever of you," Devil Eyes says. "I suppose I should be very impressed."

My friend's legs are slightly bent. We're going to chase the ball soon. We're going to push. Win. I stand up, more determined to do it when Angela Tart tuts and tries to stop me. I stand tall and like a man, ready to do what needs to be done.

"Please," the girl says, desperate to win the ball, the ceremony, the talking dog. My head. She raises her claws. "Just give us the keys and let us go."

"I'd listen to her. This is very, very foolish, Charles."

"Leave her here with us," my friend says.

"You heard her. She wants to come with me. Maybe we're lovers."

"Just—" My friend pretends he's going to keep arguing, and then *throws* himself at the devil. It's something of almost biblical proportions, as if my friend is wilfully diving into the belly of a whale. I've seen him do that tackle countless times, and so I do what I always do, as a forward. I rush around the coffee table.

My friend's knees land on the table and partially flips it, but he's got his arms around the devil's waist. The devil is laughing as he reaches down, meaning to separate the hands, and then, instead—like inflicting pain is more important—he grunts and *hits* my friend. Right on the head. What sort of move is that? I shout and throw a left hook like the older boys taught me in a muddy field near the YMCA. He grunts and stumbles, dragging my friend with him.

"Hit him again," my friend growls.

I hammer him with my right hand. My friend drives him against the wall. I keep swinging my hands, but the devil takes them, laughs, and then finally bucks my friend away and sends him sprawling to the floor. I swing one more time – too fast, he ducks, his hands are wrapped around my throat, squeezing so hard. I feel my bone matter crackling and shifting around. And I know it was going to end here, always; there was never a way out of this. Devil Eyes was always going to complete his ceremony.

"Everybody dies," he says manically, holding me one-handed as he flares out with his other hand, backhanding my friend so hard he goes flying right into the display unit. "Everybody…" Devil Eyes squeezes me harder. "Dies." The lights are dimming – I'm sitting in the theatre with Polly and both of us are laughing because we've decided to hang around instead of waiting in the cold for our bus. Nobody's checked, and she's too shy to kiss me, and I'm too shy to kiss her. "Everybody… *Ah!*"

Suddenly, he lets me go. I drop to the floor, shocked my head is still attached to my body. My neck burns and when I let out a breath, it's like wind through broken glass. I'm in so much agony I even welcome Angela Tart's touch on me.

Devil Eyes turns – and the feral girl stabs him, clearly for the second time if his stumbling gait and my ability to breathe is any indication. This thrust catches him in the shoulder. That's Polly's favourite knife. It *was*. Sharp and Japanese and expensive. She always used to brag about that knife, and I'd tease her for it.

"Bitch!" the man roars.

She lashes out at him again, catching him in the arm. Then my friend leaps from the floor and grabs his legs, shocking him toward the floor. The woman screams and leaps down at him – and then Satan summons power straight from Hell. He roars and kicks out at my friend, using the momentum to carry him toward the door.

"Run!" the feral girl screams, chasing after him. But my friend doesn't listen. He chases after *her*. Shaggy yaps from the corner, tail tucked between his legs.

"Oh, dear," Angela Tart whispers. "I need to ring the police."

I touch her hand. Maybe she's not with them after all. She'll never replace Polly, but maybe I could learn to tolerate her, maybe even like her. I'd never love her. But perhaps I could make more of an effort. She feels warm and reassuring. "You're doing your best, Angela," I tell her.

She smiles, looking like she might sob, then climbs to her feet and moves toward the phone.

34

HIM

Oh, this is good. This is real. My shoulder is injured and in serious pain. I can feel my muscle throbbing as I run into the dark. The first attack missed anything vital in my back, but my rear deltoid feels like it's taken a deep cut. The one on my arm is superficial. Oh, this is *good*. Maybe this all does end in prison. It'll be hilarious if it doesn't, a real indictment of the state of policing in this country. But for now, I run down the street, scanning the houses. I haven't got long.

I spot a detached bungalow, small, probably only housing one person. As I stalk closer, a security light comes on. I ignore it and pick up my pace, walk around the side of the house, my head feeling light from the blood loss. I need a first-aid kit, alcohol, something to stop the bleeding. My body is otherwise okay. Ready to go.

A window is open at the side, cracked a few inches. I pry it the rest of the way and then carefully pull myself inside. People would be surprised by the close confines a man like me can fit into. It's about body positioning and spatial awareness. I *do* fall toward the end, but that's just because of my bleeding face.

Suddenly, a light switches on. Oh, how pathetic. Jesus Christ.

What a joke. A woman with red frizzy hair and a pale complexion is holding a *fly swatter* in one hand and what appears to be some kind of air freshening spray can in the other. In slow time, I can see the transition register on her face. She's gone from playacting preparation because, of course, nothing bad *really* ever happens… to being greeted with a huge, blood-covered ghoul of a man.

I can't help it. I spring up. Grin. "Boo."

After efficiently and quickly killing her, I check the cabinet for a first-aid kit.

35

KATY

"You just relax, sweetheart," Charles says, standing at the kitchen window with a knife in his hand. I thought they might have a firearm. Charles does, apparently, but he doesn't want to leave us to collect it. Not until the police are here. "It won't be much longer now."

I can't stop shaking. It was like I'd gone on autopilot, first saying all that twisted stuff to convince him to leave – it *was* just twisted stuff, I think, I hope. I can't be grateful to him even in the most disgusted and head-fuck way. And then, after that, running into the kitchen, grabbing the knife, sprinting back into the living room just in time to stab him in the back.

"Are all the doors locked?"

We're in the kitchen because it has the strongest door, apparently, with two bolts. We've propped a chair against the other door. Charles *frowned* when I asked him to do this. I get the vibe that he thinks this is all done and dusted now the police have been called. It's evil, disgusting, but *manageable*. "Yes, dear, they're all locked."

I grip the knife harder, shivering when I hear sirens. I can't let myself believe it's really over. He's out there somewhere.

Everything he does is logical. Pain won't stop him. There won't be any shock about what's just happened. It's been five, ten minutes. Is that enough time for him to do something? The sirens sound woefully far away.

In the corner of the room, in what appears to be Martin's usual seat, Polly sits with him, dabbing at his neck with a wet warm towel. "Thank you, love," Martin says, and Polly shudders, flushing with something like pleasure.

"How much longer?" I ask.

"If we can hear them, not long," Charles replies. "We'll just—"

I scream when the window shatters, a rock smashing through. A voice comes from the dark a moment later. "Read the note, read the note, read the note."

Looking down, I see what he means. He's curled up a piece of paper and bound it to the rock with an elastic band. He must've had zero hesitation.

"Before the police arrive!" he calls. "Hurry, Katy!"

"Leave it," Charles hisses at me, but I can't.

I grab the rock, uncurl the paper. There are spots of blood on it.

> You lied to me three times. First, the car tyre. Then, Polly's signal. Finally, you betrayed me. That's three lies for three lives. Run into the garden or I kill them all before the police arrive.

"What does it say?" Charles tries to snatch it, but I take a few steps away from him, and look at these people, innocent and good, with problems of their own. I can't inflict this on them. I cut him *badly* and he's already planned ahead. I had my shot. He's got nothing to lose now.

"Thirty seconds," Markus calls from the darkness, his voice seeming to come from everywhere.

"Shut up, coward!" Charles roars back, then lowers his voice. "Listen, darling, whatever he's done, whatever thoughts he's put into your head, don't listen, all right? Hear those sirens?"

"Fifteen seconds." Even after being stabbed, he still sounds calm, like he's simply stating a fact. There's no hesitation and second guessing. He doesn't even care if he gets caught.

"I'm sorry." I back away to the kitchen door, my footsteps crunching over the glass. "I'm so sorry."

"Stop," Charles yells, but I throw the door open and sprint into the dark. I don't get further than ten feet before a powerful arm springs as if from nowhere and pulls me close to him.

"Stupid bitch," Markus growls in my ear, pulling me into the dark, past an apple tree, over a fence – he grunts and pushes me to go first – and then across a field. He wrenches my forearm so hard I can feel my shoulder almost popping out of the socket. All I can do is keep jogging after him so he doesn't seriously hurt me. I had the knife when I ran – I've dropped it. I've failed so many times, and maybe this is one more, but at least those people are alive.

The sirens get louder behind us. Markus groans as he climbs over a fence then turns, gesturing at me. The fence is between us. The sirens sound close. The house – this is my chance. All those moments I wondered, thought I *should* do something. But he's made a mistake. He should've made me go first, like the first time.

I turn, start running.

"Fuck," he grunts from behind me.

Looking over my shoulder, I see him vault himself one-handed over the fence, his silhouette moving athletically. He lands in an infuriatingly easy crouch and then ducks his head and runs after me *fast*. It's shocking, and, shamefully, I turn and start pleading with him. I slide on the wet grass and moan up at him. "Please, I'm sorry. I'm sorry."

"Stop messing me about."

"I'm sorry."

"Hurry *up*." He casually kicks me in the leg. "Now."

I stand up, running ahead of him when he waves a hand. He shoves me when halfway climbing over the fence, sending me heavily to the ground. The impact sends harsh reverberations through me. Climbing to my feet, I moan in pain when he grabs my arm and wrenches me toward the dark.

"Goddamn sirens," he snaps. "You've really fucked me, Katy. It'll be prison for me. But not before the night is done. The night is all that matters. *The night*. I swear to you, God, if you send me a vehicle, I'll take back every bad thing I've ever said about You. I'll pray to You every day for the rest of my life. I'll love You. Please, God."

He sounds desperate… but not desperate for the regular reasons people would in this situation, even bad people. He sounds like an artist on the verge of tears because a terminal illness is going to take him before he can finish his masterpiece. We walk through a small wooded area, coming to a road.

"Please run," he says to me, not God, then lets me go and actually *kneels* beside the road.

He'd probably be happier if this story ended with him catching me, then beating me to death before surrendering to the police.

"God, help me. Please, help me."

36

HIM

It takes a truly desperate man to resort to prayer. I was going to take the fly-swatter lady's car, but I couldn't find her goddamn keys, and then I heard the sirens. This road would be better to flee by, anyway, if I had a vehicle. But there's no point simply running into the countryside without wheels. Maybe I could find somewhere to hide for the night. I've roughly bandaged my stab wounds. The light-headedness is almost tolerable.

From behind me, I can *feel* Katy watching. I want her to run, honestly. At least that would slot the puzzle piece into place. I could just kill her now, but corpses have never interested me in the way they do to the weirdos in the films. Playing with body parts, sniffing them, *woe is me Mummy never loved me.* Those kinds of killers are pussies. The process is what interests me.

"God, I'll forgive you for my father's lies. I swear it."

I pray some more, maybe making a fool of myself, but it's not like that matters when it's only Katy. Finally – after minutes – I stand, turning to find Katy with her hands clasped across her middle, her eyes gleaming in the streetlights. Let's see how much she's *really* willing to play this game, then. She fooled me before, slightly, just a tiny bit. I won't let her fool me even one per cent this time. But I'm fine with appearances, gleaming surfaces.

She shivers when I raise my hand and touch her face. "What do you think, Katy? Shall we end it here? Or shall we try circling back to the village and hot-wiring a car? It's much harder than they make it look on TV, but it can be done. Most likely, though…" If the world is fair, some might say. "We'll be caught. I could end it here."

She gets the message. "I don't think you planned on finishing this in the mud. Let's do this properly."

I touch her hand. She does a better job at hiding her wincing this time. To think this hand is the one that plunged the knife into my back not long ago at all. She would've been happy if I'd bled out or ran like a coward because of a few scratches. But she's finally getting the point. It's only taken four corpses to drum it into her stupid head. She sees it now. There's nowhere to fucking hide.

"Good girl," I say. "We better get moving."

I jog down the road, keeping one hand on her – the one not sliced and aching from where she cut me. I can feel how difficult it is for her to keep my pace, but I don't slow down. What a feminist I am. Ha! My spirit is returning. This is simply a new chapter in the adventure. The sirens are whining from the north-west, and we're circling around them. Ideally, I'll take us to the other side of the village. Will they cordon it off? Hopefully the man in charge isn't ex-Met, like Charles. A nice, slow country bobby will do me.

The bitch trips and makes a noise of panic, a note in it like she thinks I'm going to stop. But I'm done playing nice with her. I pick up my pace and leave her to either catch her feet or sacrifice her arm. She squeals and cuddles up close to me. I almost think she's trying to seduce me, and I almost laugh, thinking of *the night*, everything I had planned. I was going to show her who she really is.

We move for minutes, and then a remote farmhouse comes into view, on the outskirts of the village. There's a jeep out front. It looks on the older side, far better for this kind of thing. I approach the building from the rear, then crouch behind a short wall, keeping the bitch at my side. She makes animal-like moaning noises so I hit her in the belly. I do it with my bad hand, the one attached to the wounded arm. The slut. I hit her again, holding her in place with my other hand. The useless whore.

"Please." She gasps.

"Shut up. No more noise. Follow me. Silently. If anybody appears, don't get involved."

I drag her over the short wall, crouching as I approach the car. There's an American-style door, wire grating, separating the porch from the interior of the house. A security light switches on. Upstairs, I hear a voice, a questioning tone. *Did you hear that?* maybe. But it doesn't matter. I almost cheer. I believe in You, then, you bastard. I see You just like my father did. Just past the wire-grating door, there's a hook with a key on it. What sort of lunatic leaves their keys in such a vulnerable place? Was it a mistake? Or did God move them?

I'm chuckling now, as I drag Katy to the door and kick it in. It snaps open and I quickly grab the keys, not even feeling the pain in my arm anymore. Everything feels distant and dreamlike. Maybe it's the blood loss working to my advantage. I move like a lazy but swift beast, no wasted motion, grabbing the keys, walking quickly to the car, unlocking, shoving the bitch inside. Footsteps, pounding, somebody messing with the door, the sound of metal. But I'm already in the driver's seat, a smile on my face, wondering if it's true. If Dad was right. The pervert. The monster. If he was right about God.

Speeding down the road, I start planning ahead. We'll need to change cars soon. We'll need to avoid all motorways and preferably stick to country roads. We'll need to take an unclear course to our destination… but *one night*. It's only two am. There's time. By the time the sun rises, Katy will be a different person.

"I'm sorry for being so rough with you," I tell her, as I push the car past sixty, taking a corner so fast I would've killed anybody coming the other way.

"It's okay," she whispers, sitting up and pawing at her bloody nose.

I don't remember hitting her in the face. But it's not like I always remember or even pay attention to every violent thing I do. Driving, that's the only thing that matters. Do I even need to switch cars? If I avoid surveillance, their options will multiply, requiring more resources. They won't find me *tonight*. I wonder if that's worth the risk, perhaps just for the thrill, knowing any moment it could all come crashing down. This is so much better than all the others.

"Really," I tell her. "I didn't want to hurt you. That's not what this is about. I lost my temper."

"I can kind of guess why…"

She lowers her hand, bloody and half broken, but she smiles. She manages that, in the midst of all this. That's reason enough to make this work. She deserves to see where this ends: deserves to learn who she really is, what she's really capable of. She's spent her life never knowing. Even after that pathetic little *incident*, she didn't know. She's the most interesting woman yet. They all have secret alleyways and beautiful corners of their minds, their souls, from an aged dignified older woman to a shy schoolgirl. They're all such wonderful creatures.

"You look happy," she notes, in a calm voice, putting me at ease, honestly, even if I know deep down she hates my guts. But she won't for long. Fuck Martin and Polly – *Polly* – and that up-his-arse copper. They were never a part of this. I got sidetracked. Not anymore. I'm driving with a purpose. They won't catch me before I eat this woman's heart.

"I am," I tell her. "I've rediscovered my relationship with God."

I think she might kick up a fuss when I take another tight corner at seventy miles per hour. It's like I can sense her worrying back there, intent on disturbing this new good mood. But then she blossoms like a flower and replies, "That's fascinating. When?"

See, this is all surface. But she sounds so perfect when she talks in that sweet feminine tone. When I planned this night, I wasn't sure if I would enjoy this next bit. I'm not even certain now. But the chances seem higher.

"Just now. The keys were right there, in the light. I prayed to God for a car. But He couldn't make it simple for me."

"Do you really believe that?" she asks, ruining her good track record.

"With all my heart. I've been religious on and off all my life. It's strange. I can simultaneously know that religion is a crutch for weak men and also that God is realer than you, Katy, or me. He's the realest thing. I'm not sure if that's a sign of an emotionally mature individual or a madman." I let myself laugh, thinking of all the helpful chemicals it releases in the human body. A magical thing, humanity. A *godly* thing. "God's going to take us to where we need to go. Katy. Poor Katy. Perfect Katy. We're going to make this night *the night*. Together."

37

KATY

Where are the police? We drove out of earshot of the sirens at least twenty minutes ago. Markus navigates the road with a psychopathic comfortability with speed. He seems to know all the roads in England, turning confidently, never once stopping to plan the journey.

"What's my princess thinking back there, huh?"

I resist every single reflexive impulse. No wincing, no disgusted shivers. I keep a smile on my face hoping it won't crack. Markus has changed; I'm not sure I've ever seen the real him. Now, he speaks to me like I'm his girlfriend, and he has the wide-eyed wanderlust look like religious people get.

"About your driving skill," I tell him.

I expect a sarcastic comment. He's seen through me every time I've tried to play him. But it's like he's letting me. "What about it?" he asks, somehow flirty.

"You seem to know the roads very well."

"I have the map of the entire southwest memorised. Not only that, but visualised. For weeks, I mentally drove down each road, correcting any mistakes. Do you think I'm telling the truth?"

"That's really impressive," I say. "Seriously. Not many people would have the discipline to do that."

"Do you, though? It's a sin to lie. I refuse to be a sinner."

Suddenly, he seems emotional. It's so strange. It's almost comical, like he has split personality or something. He laughs suddenly, causing me to jump, then laughs, a manic maniac. "I asked you a question," he snaps.

"Yes. Of course. You're very clever."

"You stabbed me," he says. "But Jesus said turn the other cheek. So I'm going to be good to you tonight, Katy. The police might get to us eventually, but I'm confident it will take them some time."

"What have you got planned?" I ask, as he speeds around another corner with a blind spot, doing it with the casualness of driving ten miles per hour.

"That would mean ruining the surprise," he says. "Don't worry. I think you'll like it. In fact, I *know* you'll like it."

Where are the police? It's not like I can just jump from the car. For the hundredth time on this cursed night, my mind plays slideshows of all the chances I've had. But I took *some*. If God's real, he's on Markus' side. Everything has gone in his favour. My skin crawls thinking of the place this is heading, the tone he's setting.

"Anybody would think you're trying to flirt with me," I say, trying to hide the reflexive sickness I feel at the idea.

"Don't rush this," he says. "I've got everything planned just right. But for now, just be quiet, okay, my sweet angel?"

My stomach turns. It doesn't take any effort to be quiet, because, for the next hour, I feel like I'm going to puke. I close my mouth and continually swallow, fighting the urge, knowing it will make him angry. The quiet seems to suit him. Finally, he pulls up at what looks like a farm.

"It's not much from the outside," he says, as the headlights come to rest on an old weather-beaten sign, the letters no longer readable. "I need to put you to sleep." He opens his car door and walks around to the back, throwing the rear door open.

I cringe against the opposite door, wishing I had the guts to run and the skills to make it work. But even with that injured arm, he'll catch me. He frowns, disappointed. "What's wrong with you? I thought you were *excited*, Katy?" The real Markus – or, at least, the usual one – comes through on the *excited*. But then he turns weirdly sincere again. "This is for your own good. I've got everything set out just right. But first I need to choke you unconscious."

"Ma-Markus," I whisper. "Please."

"Don't start that," he says. "I'm not going to hurt you. You'll be out in three seconds. And when you wake up, you'll feel so, so happy."

Tears sting my eyes. So useless. But they come anyway. "You wanted to teach me to see things clearly, remember? Well – let me ask you clearly. Are you going to rape me, Markus?"

He scowls. "Please don't use such melodramatic language. You'll understand what I mean soon. If you don't let me put you in the chokehold, it's going to have to get ugly. Come on. Be reasonable."

I rub the tears from my cheek. There are no options to weigh. I'm going to have to… Can't I run? But I've tried running. There's nowhere to go. I should fight him, make him kill me. But my life matters, doesn't it? Mum and Dad would be sad. My work friends would probably care. I'm such a lonely person. If I get out of this, I need to change that.

"Katy."

"How would it work?" I ask.

"You know, Mrs Brazilian Jujitsu. I'll put you in a rear naked choke. You'll be out in two seconds with my squeeze. Come here."

Distancing myself, it's like I watch myself make the stupidest decision of my life. But it seems like the only one. I crawl across the seat, step into the cold night air, and then turn and allow him to wrap his bulky arm around my neck and cradle the back of my head with his other hand. He squeezes me against him. My instinct is to tap, which makes him chuckle as he keeps squeezing, crushing my neck, and then, nothing, darkness. Part of me wishes it would stay dark.

When I open my eyes, everything is warm. It's like I'm floating in a giant bath. I lean back, letting the comfort slide over my muscles. Light shimmers across the room, petals of it blossoming and sparkling across my vision. I'm in some kind of dining room, no windows, just wallpaper and four lamps. My arms feel like wings pressed against my sides, stopping me from flying away. I look down… is that my red dress? I don't remember buying a dress like this.

Layers of rope wrap around my middle, holding me in place. Behind me, I hear Markus sigh, and it makes me want to smile, a human sound, a male sound, husky and appealing. Everything is so, so, so warm. Like the world is cuddling me. And I want to hold the world.

"Finally, you're awake." He walks around the table, wearing a suit that fits him well, his hair swept to the side, his different-coloured eyes glinting with a thrill for adventure. It's like he's inviting me to come on some epic journey with him. "How are you feeling?"

"Yeah – uh – not bad…"

He smiles like I'm his most well-behaved pet, and I feel proud. On some level, I know I should drag this pride through the dirt and kick it in its teeth and scream in its face and make it suffer like the foolishness it is. But on another – warm and floaty and oh-so tingly – I don't see the problem with it. I've spent this evening constantly scheming, thinking, but now I can just sit back, nothing. Obliterated.

He sits beside me, too close. I've got ropes around my body. I feel demented, like that old man. *Fucked in the head.* It's like Markus' voice is in my mind. I'm not usually so callous, am I? I want to cry and laugh at the same time. He leans in, bringing the scent of cologne with him. Slowly, I remember the details of before, the choking, the darkness, the police…

"How long?" I ask. "Where?"

"Hush, pretty petal," he says, in a tone which is somehow soothing. "Everything's going to be okay." He extends his hand, strokes it across the back of my cheek. I lean away from him, though, truthfully, he feels warm, weirdly inviting. "You don't have to worry anymore. The police. That nastiness in that pathetic little village. None of it. Now it's just me and you."

"I thought you didn't want me… like that."

He frowns, the pride burning into disappointment. *Uh-oh, I've made Dad angry.* That's what I think, how sad. It's not like Dad was ever cruel to me. He'd certainly never drag me through a muddy field, almost breaking my arm, kick and punch me. I try to focus, try to hate.

"Is that an issue?" he says, sliding his hand across the table… gripping the shiny polished hilt of a steak knife. He gently presses the point of the knife into the table and then spins the blade around. It rushes quickly, showing me tiny snippets of my reflection, like little stolen pieces of my soul. "Katy? Focus. Is it a problem if I'm romantically interested in you?"

"Yuh-yes."

"What's with the goddamn stutter?" he snaps, letting the knife drop as he bolts to his feet, walks quickly to the other side of the table, bad energy radiating from him. It's like he has to get some distance or he'll hit me. But it doesn't bother me. He turns, stares. "Well? You stabbed me and I'm still able to speak. You're acting like that R-word you really don't like me using. See? I'm being polite, *nice*. Tell me about your stutter."

"I don't know," I whisper.

"What do you mean – you don't *know*? How couldn't you know?"

"I had a stutter when I first started talking, apparently. My parents just left me alone. They were patient. It began to fade naturally on its own. Mostly, I'm okay. But when I'm stressed…"

"So I make you *stressed*." He runs a hand through his hair. "You're really not trying very hard, are you? I wonder if you could think of something nice to say if your life depended on it." He returns to the chair, seeming amped-up, his eyes wide and alert. *High*. Is he stoned? He reminds me of my coked-up friends from uni, yelling about shots and songs with hands that never stopped moving and more gums than teeth. "The stutter… you know, as an intelligent woman, that it had to have a reason. There's always a reason. Maybe Daddy diddled you and you forgot about it."

"Sometimes, it's better not to overthink things," I tell him. "And for the record, nothing like that ever happened."

"Better not to overthink… coming from a *counsellor*."

"I counsel people not to overthink all the time."

He sits back, seeming dissatisfied. I don't know what he wants from me. Everything is too slow and honest and cloudy. He's hinting at sex – no, rape, rape, fucking *rape* – but I'm getting no signals from him. He seems muted. Almost like he's trying to force me to turn the volume up for him.

"These nine men, then," he says after a pause. "You've opened your legs nine times for nine men. How many of them were casual encounters?"

"Why does this matter?"

He slams his hand on the table, then shivers strangely. It's like there's an evil spirit in him trying to break out. "*Because I said it matters*," he roars, but there's nothing behind it. He's just artificially made his voice loud.

I just stare at him, indifferent to the outburst. He leans over, grabs the steak knife again. "It matters because I want you to know how much more special it's going to be with me. We have a connection. I've touched your underwear, lain in your bed. I've thought about using that body of yours for a long time."

"I think you're lying," I say. "I think, for some reason, you're trying to work yourself up to doing this."

"Oh, Katy… you think I need to work up to doing *anything*? I'm capable of forcing myself through any series of motions, regardless of how grotesque or immoral it might be. I could detach myself from my body and instruct it to take you. It wouldn't be pretty. I've never done it before. I would prefer for it to be more intimate than that. But I could do it."

I don't even feel the urge to flinch. I just stare at him. There is no me – only him. It's like, after all these years of trying to understand people, I've finally learned the secret. "I could detach myself too. I did it before. During… the *rape*. That word means nothing to me. Go on, then. Do it that way. We'll both detach. We'll watch as these fleshy vehicles smash together. Do it, Markus. Or whatever your name is. *Do it*."

38

HIM

We're fifteen feet underground, in the dining room I have used several times before. But those times, I never entertained the idea of making love to the women. There's something different about Katy, entirely unrelated to her physical appeal. It's her grit, her calm. That's why I should've anticipated this. The drugs I gave to the others – the cocktail that made them nauseous and compliant – is having a surprising effect on her.

It's like she's looking straight through me. Even tied to the chair, even in the dress I put her in – so she must know I've seen her naked – she just watches me. Not puffing herself up, like before. Not scared. A calm, patient animal. I believe her; I could do it, take her, and she'd let me, and it would mean nothing.

"I'm not a beast," I tell her. "I've never done that to a woman. And I never would. In fact…" Why am I telling her this? Maybe it has something to do with the stimulants pumping around my body, a necessity due to my stab wounds. I'd be good for nothing otherwise. "I've never slept with anybody."

"You're a virgin?" she says, sounding genuinely interested.

I toy with the steak knife again, but it gets no response, not even a small one. I wonder if I gave her too much. But at least there's not all that blubbering emotion now. I'm wasting time, talking with her. I should do this then take her to the end. That will prove who she really is. Let God decide. *God.* I'm nobody. Not a religious zealot and not a devout atheist and nothing in-between. A nameless man. A soulless man.

"Yes," I reply, after a long pause, during which she just sits there disinterestedly, unlike before when she was sticking eagerly to my every word.

"Why?" she asks.

"Isn't it obvious?"

"Your mum's job."

"I tried to have sex with a girl when I was fifteen. I did a good job, back then, of showing people what I wanted them to see; I was an early bloomer in that regard. This girl liked me. She said she wanted to go all the way. So I tried… and I couldn't see her as anything but a dirty slag. When we started kissing and she was moaning… I spit in her face and left. Nobody believed her. I spread rumours about her to shut her up."

"That's extremely cruel and manipulative," she says plainly.

"Ever since then, I haven't been able to do it. But I think you might be different."

At the corners of her eyes, there's a slight tightening, like the sober Katy is piercing through. But then it's gone. It's not enough. "You didn't want this girl to feel pleasure."

"I didn't want to hurt her, either. But the way she was moaning… It was like all she wanted in the world was to be fucked. It was like she was addicted to dick. It was disgusting."

"Would you prefer a woman to stare at the ceiling and think of the Queen?"

"I think the only way I could do it is if the woman was feeling pain," I say, getting rewarded with another tightening around the eyes, longer this time. A quick frown she tries to wipe away. I was going to serve a meal of cold meats, try to make a date of it, but this is better; this is the way it has to be.

"Wuh-why?"

Ah, that telltale stutter. "Looking at it from a reasonable point of view, the only way I can do this is if I envision it as revenge for what my mum did. That's how this would usually work, isn't it?"

"I'm not sure it works if you're aware of it," she mutters, so stoic I almost want to drive the steak knife through her hand to make her squeal. But then, *I* made her like this.

"Do you have any idea what it's like to be nobody?" I snap. "I believed in *God* half an hour ago, maybe a little more. You get the point. And now I don't give a fuck. I'd rape God in the ass if he was here."

No reaction – nothing. That would normally get a little flutter of civilised outrage from even the most hardened person. "You don't have a personality of your own. That's why you're so effective at what you do. That's why you were able to fool me and Polly so easily. There's nothing real about you except for your desire to hurt people."

I shake my head, actually *smiling*. Who says mood swings are a bad thing? She's being extremely rude, but it's better than before, when she was caged. "You're wrong about that. I don't enjoy hurting people. I like showing women what they're capable of. Like you… I'm going to show you you're capable of enjoying sex with your kidnapper."

"You're trying to scare me," she says plainly. "You've been doing it constantly. You can't tell me you don't feed off pain when you're so desperate to make me afraid. It's all about power."

I grab the steak knife and drive it into the table an *inch* from her hand, but she doesn't even flinch. She just tilts her head and looks at me as if to say, *Are you done with your tantrum?*

"How does this end?" she asks. "Because I don't think you're going to do what you say you want to."

I interlace my fingers, lean forward. "Tell me why."

"Because it doesn't interest you in the least. You've killed women before, but you've never done that. In fact, I get the impression somebody like you would look down on the men who force themselves on women. I'm sure you've always used the fact you *don't* do it as some kind of warped justification."

I laugh darkly. Or, at least, I'm trying to be dark. I almost want the police to kick in the door just for something to happen.

"You could let me go," she says a moment later.

I tap my hand to my head. "Wow, I'm convinced. I really wanted to hurt you until you said that. Now you've completely changed my mind."

The sarcasm gets a small, judgemental frown, as if she's the perfect one. "But you could," she goes on. "I would agree to say nothing to the police."

"You can't say nothing to the police," I snap. "They always want a story. In this deranged world where I believe your blatant lie, we'd have to agree on an alternative story. You were hooded most of the time, I kept you tied up, we hardly talked, et cetera…"

"Let's do that, then," she says. "I don't want to hold a grudge against you. Actually, I quite like the idea of thinking of you out there, watching over me…"

I drop the knife, lean across the table, letting her feel my breath on her face. She's really out of it. Or maybe she's more *into* it now, into life. She's sunken deep and she finally sees reality for what it is. She'd let me rape her and not even scream, I know it, not even react. And really? *Really?* Am I going to do that scum-fuck thing? Am I going to be like them, like the perverts who used my mum and pretended she liked it when they *knew* she didn't.

I stand up, turn away from her, walk quickly from the room.

Slam the door, lock it twice, then walk down the narrow, musty hallway, reeking of dirt and shit. I push open a door and walk down a damp stone tunnel until I come to the steps, taking them two at a time, almost throwing the small trapdoor open for a sense of freedom. We're on the farm, my property, bought with a fake name, with somebody else's money.

The night is starting to slowly bleed into day. There's no sun yet, but the stars are fading in the English sky. It would be beautiful if it wasn't so goddamn boring. I pace up and down with my hands in my pockets, my body aching from the stabs and cuts, but nowhere near as much as it should. I've got too much energy and nothing to do with it. I always thought I'd be thrilled when I found a woman like Katy.

With all the others, as I coldly and pointlessly choked their fragile necks or sent them off cliffs, I dreamed of a day when I'd see the fire, or the wit, or the spark. Something. And with Katy, there's some of it there. She's stronger. She's tougher. But there's nothing in me. I'm hollow. Closing my eyes, I breathe the air, tasting the sea. We're only a mile from the ocean. From The Place. I've had time to plan this one. I chose well. Katy might make the right choice.

Or she won't, and it will be like all the other times, just another disappointment. *What are you expecting, Noah?* It's my mum's voice in my head, maybe a mixture of the stimulants and the blood loss. I rarely think of my real name. When I do, it's with her voice, her wagging finger. *Do you want me to thank you?* She's speaking like she's possessed, like she can't even perceive reality.

I'd run into the bedroom and beat up one of her customers badly. Dad was out, and now she was worried. So, so pathetically worried that Dad would find out she'd lost a few quid. *We'll lose business because of this.*

I told her, *Your business is your body. Don't you see that?*

She just sighed and nodded and told me business was business. She had taken her sickening profession as her God. I laugh, open my eyes, shake my head. As if I'm going to do that to Katy. Sometimes, I don't know who I am, nobody or anybody. There are moods and spirits and souls battling inside of me. Or maybe that's just grandiose horseshit.

I narrow my eyes, peering across to the gate. Movement, a flash of something: a uniform? I quickly stalk backward, slip down the trapdoor with the movement I've practised so many times. The top of the door is covered in grass and leaves and layers of brush stuck on there, melting it into the surroundings. Down two or three steps, I wait, listening.

Yes, they're up there. This isn't a hallucination. I can hear the tinkling of metal and the squeak of leather boots against the earth. They pass right above me, heading for the farmhouse, not bothering to stop and look at this random patch of ground. I wait, staring at the door, ready for whatever comes. But maybe there's still a chance…

Minutes pass with more movement. And finally, a man's voice. "Nothing, ma'am."

I move closer, listen hard. Most people aren't aware how powerful their senses truly are. With diligent practice, a regular man can have hearing like a blind one. You simply have to *force* yourself to practice what seems like, for dozens of hours, a pointless skill. "Is the car there?"

"Right where you said it'd be."

"The car's computer says it stopped moving fifty minutes ago. They must be nearby."

Walking backward slowly, I turn, making no noise, and then walk down the hallway with a skip in my step. I was *just* thinking I wanted the police to arrive, and here they are, almost like all that stupid God stuff wasn't so stupid after all. When I open the door, Katy's still wearing her *I'll try to seduce* him face.

I walk over to her, lay my finger against her lips. “Don’t worry about that anymore. Honestly, Katy, I think I’ll die a virgin. I’ve been a fool. I’ve been a self-indulgent, pouting idiot. We can still have our moment. I can still show you who you are. You just have to trust me. Do you?”

39

KATY

He looks at me, all teeth, his eyebrows raised. Maybe it's the drugs – he *has* to have given me something – but it's like his skin is the leathery material of some old-timey mask. I keep thinking I can glimpse the real him, but the fact is, there *is* no real him. Despite all his preparation, he's like a toddler living in the moment, swept along by whatever deranged mood grips him. I was an idiot for thinking I could win him over, even with my body.

"You do trust me, don't you?" he says. And then he mutters to himself, "I suppose we could end it right here."

"I trust you," I say as quickly as I can, my words annoyingly sluggish.

I'm almost certain he dosed me. It occurred to me when he was doing his whole *convince me to rape you* routine. My slowness is a real problem. I'm not sure how I can fight back. I just have to go along with whatever he's got planned.

"Good." He leans over, starts untying my rope. "Because you're going to have to let me carry you. You're my burden, my penance. I'm going to carry you. And then you'll see, Katy. You'll see who you really are."

Cold wind licks at my face as he carries me up the hill. I've got my head up, looking over his shoulder, seeing lights crisscrossing below us. I wonder if they'd hear us if I screamed… But there's a gag in my mouth. There's nothing I can do. My limbs feel so pathetically weak. I hold on to his neck, testing my grip, but he just chuckles.

"It all stopped meaning a damn thing to me a while ago," he says. "But please, try something."

I want to ask him where he's taking me, how he's going to show me who I *really* am, whatever that means. The lights are getting further and further away. Then one of them turns toward the hill, toward *us*. It's not strong enough to light us up, but I feel its glow against me. Markus pauses, turns. "Fuck's sake."

He spins back up the hill and starts moving quicker, causing me to bump against him. How does he see the light change? It was so subtle, just for a moment. And he just paused like a wild animal. He doesn't sound afraid as he runs up the hill. There's no panic in his hard breathing, just the measured exertion of a machine.

Finally, we crest the hill. I twist in his embrace, met with a view of the ocean that looks endless and beautiful. The stars are glittering brightly across it, far brighter than they have any right to be, considering why we're here. There must be a reason. But all I want to do is stare at the stars and the water until I sink into them.

He takes me right to the edge and lowers me onto the rocky grass, facing the ocean. My body is so exhausted, the chemicals so warm, I can't even summon the energy to stand up. He kneels beside me, running his fingers through my hair. Shamefully, more warmth tingles through me. After the night I've had, this is exactly the sort of comfort I need. But not from him.

"Look at the ocean, Katy," he says, pulling the gag from my mouth. "Can you hear it too? The tide?"

"Yes." It crashes below us, seeming to make the whole cliffside tremble.

"It's the highest tide of the month," he goes on. "The waves are taller now than they'll be for a while. Just like you, Katy. Taller now than you've been for years. Even before *the incident*." He keeps stroking his hand through my hair, and I keep savouring the warmth even if I know I shouldn't. "I've got a simple choice for you to make."

"Jump off," I say. "See if I survive. Then you'll know if Daddy was right."

His hand tightens, grabbing a fistful of my hair. The pain is far less severe than it should be. He twists me around, forces me to look at him. His mismatched eyes are as bright as the stars. "Do you think you're clever, guessing that?"

I don't rise to his violence. That's all he is. An impulse machine, playing whack-a-mole with people. All he wants is an input for an output. He was stupid for dosing me with these drugs. They've allowed me to see him for the nothing he is.

"It's obvious," I tell him. "I don't think you have any sincere, true desire for anything specific. But you must be curious about your father's belief system. We're on a cliff. It's not a difficult leap. No pun intended."

He loosens his grip on me. "Ha, ha, ha. Hilarious and brave when you're full of gear, aren't you, Katy?"

"That's not my fault. You wanted to drug me up so you could rape me."

"I was never going to—"

"And now you've jumped to another silly scheme. You're the big bad wolf, without a name, everything planned ten steps ahead. But why? What's the point? You don't care. None of it means anything to you. Even this is silly and nonsensical. If I jumped from this cliff and survived, it wouldn't prove anything."

"If *you* made the choice, if *you* jumped because you *believed* you'd survive—"

"Listen to yourself. You sound idiotic. There's no logical connection there."

He kneels in front of me, glancing over my head, then looking down like a teacher correcting an unruly student. "I've given the others a choice similar to this. Drive into a wall at one hundred miles per hour, if you survive, et cetera… but it never worked. *They* never chose to do it. But you will. I know you're strong enough."

I should hide my disgust, play the game some more. But the game ends with me dropping to my death. I don't even care if it's the drugs. It feels good to be able to say what I really think. It's like, with more sunlight bleeding into the world, I can let more honesty bleed into me. More light.

"It's not about strength. You must know that this makes no logical sense. You're too smart *not* to know."

"Stand up. Jump. And there's a chance you'll survive. If you *don't* jump you're going to die anyway."

Not if the police get here first. Does he know I've seen them? At least, I assume it's the police. It has to be, right? Or maybe we're on private land, trespassing, and it's just the farmer coming to check on us. I won't have any chance then. Markus will kill him just like he killed the paedophile and the parents and so many others.

"This is a big decision," I tell him. "Are you going to rush me?"

"It's almost daytime," he says, making me think he *doesn't* know I spotted the lights. Maybe he thinks my eyes were closed? Or maybe his injuries and whatever stuff he's on is catching up. "This has to happen at night."

"That sounds superstitious."

"We're going to see if there's such a thing." He hooks his hands under my armpits, making me think of my jiujitsu classes, fighting for this exact position. But it all seems so far away. *She* seems distant, me. He leads me to the edge of the cliff. The closer we get, the more energy seeps into my muscles. It floods me to the point I can dig my heels in and push against him.

"Finally, she's awake."

I look down at the ocean, the waves crashing, glinting in the star light and moonlight. "I'm not jumping, Markus."

"My name is Noah," he says, all grandiose, trying to make it seem significant.

"I don't care what your name is. I'm not jumping. You'll have to kill me."

"You say that as if it's some difficult thing," he mutters. "What do you think happened the other times the women wouldn't choose?"

He stands beside me, his arm wrapped over my shoulder, his other hand on my wrist. I've only got one hand free. Any sudden motion and he can instantly send me soaring into the air. It wouldn't take much. I try to make myself heavy, sit back, force him to support my weight. Maybe I can slip to the ground, crawl?

"This is different," I tell him.

He sounds amused. "Oh yeah? How?"

"You're bored. You don't want to keep repeating the same thing over and over and over."

"That's why you have to jump," he snaps.

"But I won't. So you'll have to kill me. Which you've done before. You're going to drive yourself insane with boredom."

He guides me closer to the edge. Small stones kick away as I try to dig my heels in, toppling over the edge. Beneath us, the sea rages almost like it's hungry, like it's been waiting for me. I lean against him, the only thing stopping me from falling.

"Oh, Katy," he says. "You're right. I won't lie. This all seems so regular to me. What does that say about me, the fact *this* feels routine? I know, I don't want you to answer that. But people – how do they live? How do they stomach regular existence?"

"Letting me go would be new," I whisper.

"Sure, a novel idea. But then what? Prison?"

"If you push me, you'll go to prison anyway. The police will be here soon."

He stiffens against me. "So you did see them. Yes, I'm sure they'll be with us any minute. And you're right. A murder here means prison time for me. And anyway, you might survive. I'd usually choke you before I threw you over the edge, just to be sure, but I don't think I have the time for that."

"Let me go and I'll tell them any story you want me to."

"I'm not going to fall for that. And anyway, your story won't matter. I've made too much noise tonight. If they haven't found Roger's parents already, they will. Not that they *deserve* to be found. For raising and forgiving their rapist son, they deserve to rot."

"But I *won't* jump," I tell him. "It wouldn't prove anything. This is just madness, plain and simple."

"Do you think I'm mad? Really?"

"No," I admit. "And that's the worst part of all."

"Ah, here they are."

Suddenly, he spins me around, putting himself on the cliff edge and holding me in front of him. Several lights glare at us, almost blinding me despite the soft glow of sunlight. We're in a strange in-between place, like purgatory. My eyes adjust and the officers come into focus. There are SWAT with rifles aimed and a man wearing body armour over a shirt, making me think he must be a detective.

"Stop!" he yells. "Don't move!"

When Markus laughs, crazily, I feel a surge of hope. If he

finds this interesting even for a few minutes… is there a way out? Can I time it properly? I'd have to loosen his grip on me and shove him backward as hard as I can all in one quick, violent motion. It would mean almost certainly killing him. Oh well.

I get ready, making myself limp, visualising the movements, as he aggressively stuffs the gag back in my mouth.

40

NOAH

Well, how entirely pointless this whole endeavour has been. Not just this night, I realise, but many after the first, say, two women. The first two failures. I should've learned then that all women will disappoint when pushed to the very edge. Just like it was when I killed my father, beat his head in with a fake-gold Jesus ornament, hit him until I felt my hand breaking from the impact, and Mum found us, screamed at *me*, hated *me*.

I can feel Katy all tight against me, perhaps getting ready for one of her wannabe kung fu moves. The police are all around us, but they must know how screwed they are. The *police*. Some people respect them. I get it. The scared and weak and those who literally could not fight off an attacker themselves, they need the pigs. But how can any capable man look at an out-of-shape lump of lard like that one over there and have *respect*?

A presumable detective steps forward, flashlight raised. "Let's talk about this."

"Is that what they teach you in copper school?" I call over, striving to make my voice upbeat. From the oh-so shocked shimmers running through many of their silhouettes, I succeed.

There's an air of fear around them. They must've seen what I did to that bitch to get her car.

"What's your name? Why don't we start there?"

"Do you think this is a hostage negotiation?" I laugh. "The second I let her go, you'll swarm me. You don't care if I die—"

"That's not—"

"Please, don't interrupt me."

They're all so goddamn mammalian. I've got warm-blooded Katy in my arms, blazing with her fear, thinking she's being so sneaky by playing limp. But I can feel her small mind working, her weak limbs preparing. The detective winces, a young lad, a *scared* lad. Jesus Christ. Police really have dropped in quality. Where's the grey-haired grizzled ex-soldier?

"As I was saying," I go on, making sure to keep Katy pressed close to me. They can't risk shooting. "You don't care about my life. If there was a way to put a bullet in my head without risking us both falling over the cliff, you'd do it. So let's cut the shit."

"What do you *want*, then?"

All my life, trying to figure out the answer to that question. Katy saw through me. It's not some special feat. If I spend enough time around people, they realise I'm just the shiny front of a building, no rooms inside, no lights, no conversation. Just moving the walls around and adding new structures. There's never been any want. I don't know. I wish it hadn't been necessary to murder my father, but that was his fault.

"I'd like for you to dance, detective."

From beside him, some half a woman, a pink stump of a thing, mutters, "Sir."

"Ah, look here," I go on. "We've got one of those fat women who tries to wear it as muscle."

Her mouth drops open. Oh, it's sweet. Then her professionalism tries to wipe away her true reaction. "Your remarks won't—"

The man in the jacket raises a finger, enough to shut her up.

"That's right," I call over. "Know your place, cow." I chuckle, but not in a deranged way, not in a way that would allow them to put this, put *me* in a box. They need to think they can understand me. *He must be off his head on drugs*. But even with the speed pumping through my system, I can show them what I want them to see. Make them hear the laughter of their friends in the pub. All while their heart rates are nearing two hundred and I'm not even breathing hard.

An atmosphere of confusion spreads through them. I'm fully surrounded by torchlight now, but they don't advance.

"Do you have any idea how easy it would be for me to push her over the edge?" I ask conversationally.

The little lad who's seemingly in charge almost bursts into tears at that. "I think we can agree we don't want that to happen. I'm DI Harry Simmons."

"D*I*?" I laugh, shaking my head, causing Katy to moan and shiver against me. She's still playing dead, waiting for her big resurrection moment. She would've *got* her moment if she'd simply stepped over the edge. But she had to be difficult. "Where's the DCI? You've been to the houses?"

"Hous*es*," he mutters, emphasising the end, meaning they've only been to one house.

"Fine, fine. You saw what I did to the bitch."

Harry seriously looks ready to sob. The wind whips at us, meaning he has to raise his voice. It sounds like it hasn't even broken yet. "We've seen, yes. Was that you?"

"Jesus Christ, that's a stupid question. This is what I mean. You've been to the house." I'm shouting over the wind, but careful not to let the volume interfere with my tone. I'm not going to let them box me in. Crazy. Drugged-up. Lunatic. They're not hearing that because I'm not letting them. "You'd think they'd send someone senior. How old are you, Harry?"

"You're using my name, thank you. Why don't—"

"You're coming across as very amateur right now. Don't forget how easy it would be for me. Let's say I turned, threw her – one of your men would shoot me. But it would be too late."

"Then please tell us what you want."

"I want to speak with you," I say, giving Katy's wrist a squeeze. She whines like a little baby, causing another flutter to spread through the officers. "Firstly, tell me how old you are."

He shifts side to side, all civilised. I'm so sick of civilisation. I'd rather be savage, roaming, living by the laws of the wild and the bad. I'm so tired of tutting and tea and biscuits and bake-offs and footy on a Sunday, and people. Harry finally says, "I'm thirty-two."

"So where's the senior officer?"

"He's on his way," Harry says a little testily.

"Ah, right, of course. Because you're not capable of handling this yourself. Presumably this is the part where you try to convince me you're going to give me some impossible thing. Say, immunity, money, all that shite. Am I right, lad? Or shall we let the dyke answer?"

Just like it always does, the word gets a response. The woman can't help herself. She actually *spits*. "A serving member of the Great British police, ladies and gents, and she just spit when there's a hostage's life at stake."

The lad glares at her, and I can tell the stocky stump of a woman is seething. She's thinking of all the dresses she's ever tried on, making her feel like a bollard, all the sour looks from boyfriends, all the filters she obviously applies to her photos.

"I'd like to have a conversation with you," Harry goes on. "That's true."

I ignore him, staring at the woman. "What do you think would happen if you were up here without these men to protect you, sweetheart?"

Oh, this is good. A tremor actually moves through her.

"Let me explain—"

I loosen my hold on Katy for just a moment, a second, and she springs on it like I knew she would. She sinks her hips to the ground and fights off my arm with both of hers, all while trying to force me backward. She's so much more violent than I assumed she'd be, considering the drugs. But she hits me *hard.* I almost fall – worse, almost lose hold of her…

But then I drop to my knees, make myself solid, grab her legs before she can kick away. She tries to yell but the gag shuts her up. I duck my head and, not even half a heartbeat later, a gun goes off. I keep my head low, close to her body, and then grab her and pull her on top of me, trying to peer around her. Light everywhere. She's thrashing. The gag has come loose.

"Shoot him! Shoot him! Shoot him!"

I quickly drag her against me, my arm wrapped around her neck, using the other hand to help me stand up. She keeps struggling, thrashing wildly against me, but I can feel her slowing down. The officers are *much* closer now.

"You *idiot,*" I roar in Katy's ear, shaking her violently. "You almost pushed us both over. Who fired the shot?" I call out over the officers, and see movement behind them, grey shapes, more of them. *"Who?"*

Katy screams, muffled by the gag, when I shake her again, her terror ringing out around us.

"Let's just calm down…"

"Harry, shut up. Who fired it?"

"I did," a man calls from behind a cowardly torchlight.

"All right, then swap places with Katy here," I roar at the little prick. "And just know, if me and you were put into a cage in a fair fight, I would tear your eyes out of your head and make you eat them."

"We're not doing this…" But Harry has no power here. The owner of the torchlight steps forward, a rifle in his hand.

"Sir, I'm willing to do this."

"Stand down."

"It's a miracle they didn't fall over," he goes on stubbornly, at least ten years senior to the DI. "I can't have this."

"Don't do it," Katy says, rather bravely. She's managed to push the gag out with her tongue, or maybe she's gnawed through it, the resourceful bitch. "He won't huh-huh…" She stutters herself into a sobbing mess, bursting into pathetic tears. Yet again, just like all the others, at the end. Nothing special to offer, just tears and melodrama and nonsense. Complete wastes of time. Maybe it's just a simple cliché. Maybe that's all I've been. A man angry at his mother. But no, because *those* men have sex with the women. That makes them worse.

"Lay your weapons on the ground," I say, looking the older man in the eye, ignoring Harry. "When we make the switch, you have to keep yourself between the gunmen and me. Any tricks, any sneaky stuff, I'm taking her over with me."

"I understand," the man says. "I've been on jobs like this before. I can tell you're serious."

"You don't seem scared."

He shrugs, a real old-school sort of man, as if he doesn't know what it means to be frightened, or that he sees it as self-indulgent. Baby-faced Harry takes a step forward, but then the *stump* woman ignores rank and touches his arm. A look between them: almost intimate. Oh, wow, is something going on between those two? What an odd pairing.

"Let's do it, then," I say. "I'm done with Katy anyway. Hear that, Katy? You don't have to cry anymore. You're going to make it out of this. Maybe it will make you stronger. Okay, petal?"

I keep my arm wrapped around her as the other man approaches. He looks strong, but not like me, shorter too. Either way, I'm going to do this quickly. Gun muzzles wink at me in the torchlight. Perhaps, if this is really the end – and let's face it, it seems to be, either prison or death – my efforts will have a lasting effect on Katy. A legacy of sorts. It's not as if I'll ever have children.

"Don't be rude." I give Katy a squeeze. "Say thank you."

"Thuh-thank you," she says.

The man continues to approach until he's within touching distance, then he takes another step forward, so he's brushing up against Katy.

"We'll do this quick," I tell him. "Mess me around, you'll find out."

"What on earth is going on here?" some old bugger calls from the background, far too late to make any sort of difference.

He's not prepared for how quickly I move. It's not just the speed. It's the precision and the calm. With no overthinking, fluidly, I thrust Katy away and roughly grab the man by his vest, pulling him right up against me. He yelps as I get double underhooks on him, both my arms under his armpits. I link them and squeeze him tight against me, in what's called a body lock. He can't move. He didn't expect me to hold him like this.

Finally, I'm feeling something. Just a trickle. But I know it will turn into a storm in a second. For a few floating, flying moments. Maybe this was it all along. I wasted time wondering if *their* choice would prove anything. But what about my choice? What about me?

A fat man waddles into view, face red, clearly out of breath. He's got an overconfident frown on his face, like he's annoyed they've started without him. But now he's here… it's all going to be cushy.

"I hope you're ready to die," I tell the officer pressed against me.

A shiver – but he wilfully stops it. "I'd rather not," he says. "But I'm not going to beg you."

"Good man," I say, and then I spin around and throw myself off the edge with the man beneath me. The animal response is almost overwhelming. Let him go. Flail my hands. Panic. That's what *he's* doing as we rush closer at impossible speeds. But I'm thinking about holding on to him. Let him hit the rocks first. Let's see. Let's test this, Father. Those were his last words, after I kicked his head in and stabbed him in the gut, and Mum told the police *she* did it in a frenzy because of all that nasty work. *"God will judge you for this, son."*

We slam into a rock. Turn over. Saltwater in my mouth. Something dislodges in my arm. Screaming and then I'm swallowing and darkness closes in.

41

KATY

I'm shivering in the back of the ambulance. I can't stop shaking. It's my body and it's my heart and it's everything else. I'm trying to draw in enough air with each breath, and there's a police lady here telling me to *breathe, breathe*, but I just can't. He's going to find a way to stop this ambulance. Or catch us at the hospital.

He grabbed that SWAT member and used him as a bodyboard. Turned and jumped with *intent*. I want to ask her if they've got him yet, but I can't get any words out. I thought I was doing a good job at staying calm. But when I sprung my attack, he reacted so much faster, and then I knew I was done. There was no way out. Nowhere to run or hide. He had me. But the bullet pissed him off. Or maybe, in his warped world, he thinks letting me go proves some kind of point.

I scream and lash out at the police lady when she tries to touch me. I know it's wrong. I almost want to laugh and apologise, make light of it. Try to make her see this experience hasn't broken me. But I just can't stop crying. I thought I had it there, for a second. A chance to end him. But he was too strong. I wonder what happened when he fell. It was an insane, silly plan. But nature seems to have a way of rewarding people like Noah.

"I don't understand," Dad says, several hours later, sitting beside my hospital bed. He's wearing one of his winter sweaters, looking so much like home it breaks my heart. The curtains are closed behind him. I'm not sure if I prefer that, wondering if Markus, if *Noah*, is out there. He'll find a way, even with the police officers sitting beside me. "How haven't you *found* him?"

"Roger," Mum says, touching Dad's hand, trying to calm him down.

I'm dosed up and half human as I lie here, hardly feeling like a person at all. There's too much sluggishness flowing through me. It's either that or I give into the pain and start crying again. Each moment replays in my mind. The only way to shut it up is to stamp on the whole damn thing. But Dad's right. How the *hell*?

"He's not human," I whisper.

"Katy," Mum says, still thinking she can put this into some kind of box, the order of her mind. She doesn't understand that there's no sense with Markus. That's the only way I can think of him. He was so *charming* when he was the taxi driver.

"It's true," I tell them, feeling the police officers' eyes burning into me. This is going to be a scandal, especially with how he handled it at the end, the comments he made to the female officer. It's going to be big from a PR perspective. Maybe that's a way out of this. Maybe I should use what he taught me and be as callous as him. "He's always thinking ahead. He has no feelings at all. You can't bully or trick him. He doesn't even feel pain like a normal person. I stabbed him. He just popped some pills and got on with it."

"But where is he?" Dad snaps. "You said he grabbed one of your officers and jumped."

"Yeah, some bloody trick," the male officer grumbles, tapping his pen against his notepad. "He took a man's life because he did his job. Pathetic."

The female officer nudges him. She's got a crown of grey hair and a serious, purpose-minded expression. "Can you think of anywhere he'd go, Katy?"

"Anywhere he'd *go*?" Dad stands up, paces over to the window. He looks like he wants to break something. He stood like that when he found out about the rape. It was like – and it is like – he wants the attacker to appear. He wants to slip into the skin of the defending, supporting father. But it's never as simple as that with Markus.

"Dad," I say. "They're just doing their jobs."

He turns, hands on his hips. "You heard my daughter," he tells the officer. "She cut him. That cliff… that fall – there's no way he survived that. Why are you asking her if there's anywhere he'd go?"

"From what Katy has told us, this man is an exceptionally tenacious, cunning monster. If he somehow survived, it's likely he wouldn't waste time worrying about any injuries, or panicking."

"He'd act," I say, nodding. "Yes, definitely. It's all he knows how to do. He's an impulse machine. I think he finds it impossible to sit still."

"It doesn't matter." Dad sits heavily. "He took his own life. Did the right thing."

"Roger." Mum touches his arm.

Dad catches himself. "I'm sorry. And they took your poor lad. I apologise."

"I understand," the female officer says. "Katy…"

I try to think back to the start of yesterday evening. My body is trying to drag me to sleep, but the hellfire in my thoughts won't let me. I can't sleep, can't risk seeing *him* when I open my eyes. He'll find a way into the hospital… but does he care that much?

"I don't know," I tell them. "He spoke about his family. His mother was a prostitute. His father—"

"You've already told us that, dear," the officer says.

Mum throws her hands up, one of her favourite gestures, complete civilised exasperation. "She's exhausted. She can hardly remember her own name."

"I'm sorry," I tell the officers.

"You've got nothing to apologise for," Dad says. "It's the world that should be apologising to you, Katy. First that evilness… and then this. It's too much for one person to take."

"No," Mum cuts in. "She's strong. *You're* strong, Katy. You can get through anything."

I try to let her words sink in, try to believe them with everything I have. But there's so much trying to take hold of me.

"Even if he's dead," I say. "You might never find his body. The sea could've taken it, taken him." They've all become awkwardly silent. "What? It's the truth."

"Don't think like that, dear." Dad gently touches my hand, like he thinks I might shatter into a million pieces. "He's gone. You don't have to worry about him ever again."

"We'll leave you for now," the officers say, standing and walking from the room, letting me slip into a dream. I'm back in the taxi at the start of the evening, but this time, I ask him for a tissue and he opens the divider. And then I leap through, right at his eyes, blind him, kick the back door open, sprint and run away, get a knife from some dreamland place, run back outside, make sure the job's done. I'm moaning. Distantly, I hear Mum's voice. But I can't wake up. I'm stuck here, fighting him.

42

MARTIN
FIVE MONTHS LATER

I lean heavily on the stick as Angela touches my arm. I try not to think of her as *Tart* anymore, though it's difficult sometimes, especially when she makes her annoying tutting noises, reminding me so much of my boyhood. Another lady is on my other side, the one who tries to steal my cereal bars and stops me from seeing Angela so often. Perhaps that's why she's become tolerable.

Shaggy lopes ahead of us, walking next to a small collection of people, a woman and an older couple. Old*er*, but they're pups compared to me and old Tart. Angela is talking to someone else; I recognise his voice, and it makes me feel young, though I'm not sure why.

"Five bloody months," he says. "There's no finding him now."

"The officer returned." Angela keeps her voice low, as though she doesn't want the people ahead to hear. I hope this isn't the beginning of another one of her conspiracies.

"*Returned.* The poor bloody bugger washed up cut to pieces. That lunatic tried to *surf* on his body."

"Maybe it worked," Angela says, voice all tight.

"If it did – which it didn't – he was injured, exhausted. He drowned and got washed away with the current. It's as simple as that."

They've both got pathetic, transparent hope in their voices. It's like they're praying for this mystery man to have disappeared. They've been anxious about it ever since that strange woman up ahead came to the house and told us we had to traipse up this steep hill.

"This really is a bit much," the cereal bar stealer says. Finally, something logical from her!

"We're almost there," the man says. "I think this means a lot to her, us all being here. We're the only connection she has to that night… everybody else is gone."

"Dead, mud, in the dirt," I say.

"If you like."

"She's not going to get what she wants from this," I tell them, then feel them gawping at me as if it's absurd that I'd have an opinion after they forced me to walk all the way up here. "If there was a bogeyman, he's never going to let her see him again. Or, if he does, it'll be too late. If there's a man who knows what he's doing, like a soldier, say, and he wants to kill untrained folks, then there's nothing they can do."

"Oh, please," Angela says, becoming insufferably melodramatic.

"It's true. So she would do better to embrace it. Live until he appears and takes her life. It's simple. She doesn't have to worry."

There's an uneasy silence, as though they all want to say something but they lack the courage. I'm not sure what it is, and I can't be bothered to guess. Maybe they want to tell me a home truth of some sort. Well, they can stick it. Finally, we're at the top of the hill – not a hill, a *cliff*, and silly Shaggy runs right to the edge and starts barking.

The strange girl turns, and suddenly, I remember the

conspiracy, the ceremony, the evil tricks she tried to play and the rest of it. Shaggy: the traitor. Old Devil Eyes. That's it, him, the bogeyman. I remember how his eyes burned and nobody else seemed to see it.

Angela rushes forward. The older couple seem surprised the feral girl would turn to Tart, but it doesn't shock me in the least. Twistedness like that runs deep, cuts right to the core, slices a person up and leaves little left. She was always going to reach out to Tart, the one who remembers Devil Eyes.

"Do you still think about him?" the girl says, clinging on to Tart.

"Yes," Tart responds. "Far too much, dear. You're not the only one. But it's over now. He's never coming back. Look – look at that fall. He's a *person*, Katy. He's not a monster. He's not a bogeyman. He's a person."

But I can see from the girl's aura that she doesn't believe it, the energy buzzing around her, taunting her, making a mockery of the embrace and the so-called comforting words.

I lean on my walking stick as I walk stubbornly toward them. Somebody's got to speak some sense here. The other woman follows me, cereal bars on her mind, trying to get involved when she has absolutely no idea what's happening here and couldn't possibly fit it into her deluded head.

The girl turns, smiles at me as if I'm a crippled pet who's managed to totter a few steps. True, I am gripping my cane rather hard, and I am disgustingly grateful for the woman now clutching my arm. But I've got something worthwhile to say.

"I looked into his eyes, girl. And I saw the Devil."

"That's enough!" the older man says, stepping forward, raising his hand.

"I saw him." I ignore the man and stare at the girl, letting her know without words that I remember that night, every single nuance, every detail. And – yes, I *do* remember. "You kissed the Devil. You kissed Satan. You sold your soul, girl…"

The man lunges at me. The older woman grabs him, appalled. Tart tuts and the other man, the one I feel a vague shimmer of warmth from, is suddenly standing between us. I don't care about any of the fuss. All I care about is her, the girl, staring at me through the mayhem. She knows the truth. She knows how badly she messed up that night.

"Dad, it's fine," she says. "Just relax."

Yes, of course, because she knows I'm right. I wish I wasn't. But soon, it won't matter. I've learned to enjoy this spell they've cast on me. There's something magical about knowing, soon, none of this will matter. But I *do* know, and that gives me an edge. If I wanted, I could claw myself back to… I could, anyway. I know I could. But sometimes, it's enough to simply let it all wash away.

43

KATY

I wake in the middle of the night, then laugh like a madwoman. Hearing the laughter drums home just how deranged this really is. It's a technique my therapist recommended. Me, a counsellor, and I went to a therapist. I'm a traitor. I try to laugh again, as if to make light of it all. But it fails again. Dad says I should get a dog, but I can't stand the thought of it… *him* coming back, seeing my pet, and—

Standing, knowing there won't be any more sleep tonight, I glance at the four am clock and walk through the door. At the kitchen table, I sip milky coffee and swipe on Tinder. I don't want to be alone, but I don't want to let a man get close either. I've been going on dates. Mum encouraged it, said it would be good to get out there. But I can only ever go on one. Share a smile, have a good time, then move on with my life.

Sometimes, I wonder if I'm waiting for him to show up on one of these dates. At least then, I'd know. I wouldn't have to spend the rest of my life wondering if that sick freak somehow made it. He *couldn't* have. He jumped a hundred feet. People *have* survived that. Online, there are groups dedicated to him. They post photos of possible sightings. But the police say it's nonsense. He's dead. They want to move on.

Pathetically, I can't move on. But I haven't taken the book deals or the interviews either. I've lived off my savings and done nothing, just existed in my flat, waiting, thinking about that night. I've lived it endless times since it happened; it's like it's eaten up half my years. I lived decades in that goddamn prison.

I'm being dramatic. I try to laugh again. Ha, ha, ha. But then I swipe again and I *do* laugh. *Markus*. He's twenty-nine and has a tanned face and gleaming teeth, holding a Chihuahua with a bowtie on its collar. Depressing, but hey, it's not unusual, I hear Markus' voice. *The absolute degeneration of men will never cease to amaze me...*

I put the phone down, wonder if it's worth it, going on another date. The thing is, honestly, I'm being pathetic. I survived. I was the lucky one. Roger's parents are dead. An innocent woman named Sydney Langdale is dead. A convicted sex offender – that partially made Markus a hero online. Or *Noah*. But the police still haven't worked out his true identity. It's difficult without a body. No parents of kids with mismatched eyes have stepped forward, either.

Picking the phone back up, I go to my latest Google search. *Highest falls survived*. There are countless stories. Failed base jumps. Jumps off cruise ships. The human body sometimes does miraculous things. Going to YouTube, I click a video titled, *Is He Still Out There? (Midnight Massacre!).* A young man in a shirt looking respectable is speaking with an older man wearing gym gear.

"Could a person, well, use *another* person as some sort of shield?"

"I know many of you will laugh," the stuntman says. "But we believe it *is* possible. It's unlikely. But—"

"But you're saying," the younger man says, excitement rising in his voice, a gleeful note in it. "Markus Noah could still be out there?"

They're the only names the public has. The two names he gave me. But of all the Noahs in England, none fit his description. There was talk of expanding the search to other countries, but then the case died down. People moved on. Mum doesn't say it, but I can tell she thinks I'm silly for not taking the interviews and book deals while they were hot. She often mentions, "There's still *time*, dear."

"Not to be sensationalist," the older man says. "But yes, I think we can make that claim right now. He could still be out there."

It's a big day. I've got a job at a counselling agency. I want to focus just on the job, the face-to-face, and not have to worry about booking clients or handling finances. Just show up, empathise, make notes, leave. Then I can turn my brain off the best I can. Then I don't have to think about the thing I can't *stop* – God, I'm boring myself now. It's half a year tomorrow. Half a year and I can't seem to just let it go. Even Mum and Dad are getting sick of it, I can tell, though they'd never say it. They want their daughter back. So do I.

I can hear my last person of the day being led in by the receptionist, Charlotte. "It's okay, sir. I'm sure—"

"Sure of bloomin' nothin'," a man says, his voice grizzled, sounding like he smokes several packs a day. Charlotte opens the door and shoots me a tight frown. This agency works mostly with drug addicts and homeless people, trying to help them get clean, build confidence, generally just do something rather than nothing. There's debate about how effective it is. But I like to try at least. And it's better than being left with myself.

The man shuffles into the room, looking almost sixty, seventy, with chunky brown glasses and a dirty-looking cap pulled over long grey hair. He's wearing layers and layers of clothes, giving him a bulky, strange look. He sucks on a vape pen and blows it towards Charlotte. Charlotte leaves us with a scowl, closing the door behind her.

"Please, we've asked you about that…"

"May I?" I stand, pretending to be confident, offering my hand for the pen. He grunts and gives it to me. "Thank you, Walter. That's your name, isn't it? Walter?"

"Walter," he almost yells, and I wonder if he has some kind of alcohol-related brain damage. If so, it will be my second case today, out of nine clients.

"Would you like to take a seat, Walter?"

He walks sluggishly to the chair and sits, adjusting his bulky glasses, then staring down at the floor. I sit on the opposite chair, picking up my notepad, glancing at my notes. *Begged to be seen. Won't admit to drug use. Possible case to be passed on.* They want me to decide if he needs more serious help. I can already give them the answer to that.

"Would you like something to drink?"

"No," he barks. "Told the missus out there I didn't need none of your piss water bollocks!"

He's making a fuss, but he doesn't seem aggressive. That's been the most shocking thing today: how comfortable I've been around angry or resentful men. I thought it would take me back there. But no – I feel so proud, honestly – it hasn't.

"Okay, that's fine," I say. "So, is there anything troubling…"

He looks up, smiles, his grey beard shifting. Then he takes off his glasses and keeps smiling. It can't be him. The eyes are the same colour. Both green. It can't be him. But he keeps smiling and nodding like he's reading my mind, like he knows what I'm thinking, that thin smile smearing wider and prouder.

"There's a lot troubling me, in fact, Katy."

It's *his* voice. He raises a hand when I'm about to scream. It shuts me up. I remember the violence from before too vividly, the suddenness of it.

"Please don't," he says. "I'm here to speak with you. I don't want to get melodramatic about it."

I almost lean forward, but that would mean being closer to him. He's not making any aggressive movements. He leans back comfortably, his posture no longer that of an elderly man. The beard looks real, and the hair.

"Dyed?" I say, finally finding my voice. I won't stutter in front of him. That's it, my petty pathetic promise to myself. I won't bloody stutter.

He shrugs. "Maybe this past half-year has aged me."

"How did you get in here?"

"They announced your job on the website. I hung around outside, made a fuss. They tried to take me to somebody else. But she was busy. It's good. I was going to throw a tantrum and demand to see a different counsellor anyway. You."

I shake my head, hoping I can mask the shudder which tears through me. "How the *fuck* did you survive?"

"Keep your voice down," he says coldly.

"How?" I snap, quieter, leaning in even if I shouldn't.

"Because you know what happens if you make any noise," he goes on.

"The circumstances are a lot different this time. We're in public. It's daytime. If I screamed, there would be two, three, four people in here."

"Yes, of course, and they would all rush in with entirely violent and effective intent. It would be a serious challenge to slaughter them all like pigs."

"You wouldn't get away though," I say.

He shrugs again. "Then I suppose you'll have to wager the

lives of all your new colleagues on the assumption I care about being free."

"If you didn't care, you wouldn't be here."

"You're wrong. It was simply more fun to see how long I could go on living as a free man. So far, my existence has been quite the indictment of His Majesty's Inspectorate of Constabulary. The policing in this country really has gone to the dogs, hasn't it?"

I thought the fear would cripple me. If I ever saw him again, I thought it would spear me to my seat, make it impossible to do anything. But now, I feel weirdly free. Weirdly high. Like I could scream with relief. Finally, I know. There's no more wondering. He's here. He lived.

"Maybe you're going mad," he says, as if reading my mind, with the same rear-view-mirror grin on his face that I remember. "Maybe I'm not even here. Shall I touch you, so you know I'm real?"

"I'm not going mad," I snap. "I need answers. You owe me that."

"I *owe* you?"

"If you were going to hurt me, you'd do it," I tell him. "I'd never see you. You would do it in the most effective and quietest way. Maybe I'd 'go missing' or something like that. Fine. But you haven't. Which means you're here to talk. No – to *brag*. So go ahead. Brag to me, big man. Noah. Tell me how you did it."

"Noah," he repeats, then laughs. "As if I would ever give you my real name. Or let you see my real eyes. Contacts, Katy."

"How?" I snap. "Just how?"

He yawns, stretching his arms above his head. "You've probably seen the speculation online. There have been countless videos about it. The truth is, I thought I was going to die. The second I jumped, I knew it. I thought to myself, *Well, damn, that was stupid*. The impact was far quicker than I could've imagined.

But that pig *did* save my life. We landed on a rock. The impact broke my goddamn ribs. It crushed him, and then I was in the ocean."

"Where you drowned," I say, as if that will make it real. "Everybody knows you got swept out to sea. But it was cold. You *drowned.*"

"Nope. But I should be dead. You see, there are hundreds of small crevices and caves down there. The tide swept me out, pushed me back in, pushed me deeper into a cave. It was dark and, to regular people, it would've been unbelievably terrifying. I was injured and alone. So I laid down to die."

He speaks fondly, recalling the memory.

"Go on. Tell me you prayed."

I want some kind of response from him, but he just sighs disappointedly. "No, I didn't. That was all silliness. Just like the stuff with you. All silly and misguided."

"Silly. Misguided." Blood flashes viciously across my mind. "Do you have any idea what you did?"

"Are you still doing your jiujitsu?" he asks.

"No," I lie, to spite him, as if he cares. "I hate grappling with people now. Especially men."

"Oh, Katy." He runs his hand through his beard, his conspicuously grey beard, with dirt artfully dragged through it. "You shouldn't let our night together utterly consume and dominate your entire life. You had a bad experience. Negative things happened. To let it define you is weakness and self-indulgence."

"It must be very simple for you to say that," I tell him, keeping my voice cold, not stuttering a single damn word. "You don't have feelings. You might pretend, but you don't. So, you're in the cave…"

He waves a hand, as if it's not important. "I waited there to die. But then I woke up. It began to rain. The rain let me live on a little longer, as I was able to hydrate myself. I pissed on myself for warmth. I drank the rainwater. I let my body revert to fasting mode. I've gone weeks without food before. I waited. I wondered. I began to believe I might be Jesus, you know, the cave and all that. But it was just my body telling me I'd pushed the fasting too far."

I grind my teeth, wishing it was impossible. Thinking of all the hubbub online if I ever told this story to the world.

"It turns out I'd been in there for three weeks. I learned that when I broke into somebody's house and saw the newspaper. No killing this time, no fuss. Just a few missing tins of beans. And from there, I walked the countryside, living off beans. I had a beard. I was much, much thinner than before. One of my arms was grotesquely out of place. Ha. Did I mention that part?"

"You want me to be proud of you," I snap. "How impressive. You managed to claw your way back into society. Well done, Markus, Noah, whatever your name is."

"I don't care if you're proud," he says. "I'm here because I want you to move on. I've checked in on you a few times, seen you leaving your little dates early, seen you looking lost and alone even if you're surrounded by people in a restaurant. Just let it go. It's over. I lived. I don't care about you."

"If you didn't care, why say any of this?"

He stands, adjusting his beard. I wonder if even *that* is real. "If you tell anybody I was here, bad things will happen. But if you pretend that the mad old homeless man didn't want to be counselled, I swear, you'll never see me again. No more wondering. No more fear. Okay, Katy?"

He glares at me. I feel the old, depressingly familiar fear return. "Okay."

"One more thing." He smirks. "Do you have any idea how difficult it is to break a zip tie? Even with a knife, it's tough going. I normally have to use pliers. But if you leave them in a humid room, under UV light, for a long time, they become brittle, weak… I wanted to see if you had the guts. And you did, didn't you? But you still failed. You didn't stop to think how impossible it should've been. No, as usual, you *believed* in yourself."

I stare, dumbstruck. The lunatic never stops playing games.

With that, he starts moaning and shouting, limping toward the door. Charlotte comes rushing down the hallway when he throws the door open.

"No bloody use, this'un!" Markus roars, bounding away with heavy steps. "Absolute waste of space!"

"I'm sorry," Charlotte says, looking at me with raised eyebrows, a small smile, as if saying, *Some first day, huh?*

I should say something. I should tell somebody. He's going to hurt more people. The police have to know. *Bad things will happen*. If I tell anybody, though, he'll act fast, ruthlessly. He'll hurt Mum and Dad. He might even hurt Charlotte for smiling at me and making me a coffee. Am I really going to do this, say nothing? Let him go out there and find somebody else?

Can I live with that?

44

HIM

I'm always waiting to get caught. When I was dying my beard in a public toilet at one am, I was laughing to myself, feeling like a cracked-out old man anyway from all the terrible nutrition and hard living. Even now, eight months later, I'm waiting for the police to show up. I'm living with a junkie called Thomas who thinks my name is Barry Mitchell. He's hardly with it, allowing me to keep him juiced-up in the bedroom and the rest of his flat tidy. Luckily, I got to him in the sweet spot: before the cuckoo artists moved in but after he'd rendered himself useless with drug use.

I've trimmed my beard and hair but kept it grey. I still apply subtle make-up around my eyes for the age effect, but I no longer streak dirt through my beard. This new version of me is moving on to a better life. With an arm that is always throbbing from where the fall twisted it out of place – I had to try and force it back myself – I'm starting to wonder if this new version of me could be even better.

I've even started going out in public. Showering in Thomas' flat allows me to venture into cafés, supermarkets, book shops. That's where I saw you, walking through the book shop, a look of wonder on your face. It was so simple and beautiful to follow you to your car, to find your name, to find your address. To stand outside and wonder what could be.

Maybe I'm mad for wanting to do this all over again. But I can't get you out of my head. Soon, I'll move to the next stage. Being in your home. Touching your things. Planning our future. Maybe this time, with you, it'll all be worth it. Maybe you'll finally make me feel something. I hope so.

THE END

ALSO BY NJ MOSS

All Your Fault

Her Final Victim

My Dead Husband

The Husband Trap

The Second Wife

Through Her Eyes

Ruin Her Life

The Twins

A NOTE FROM THE PUBLISHER

Thank you for reading this book. If you enjoyed it please do consider leaving a review on Amazon to help others find it too.

We hate typos. All of our books have been rigorously edited and proofread, but sometimes mistakes do slip through. If you have spotted a typo, please do let us know and we can get it amended within hours.

info@bloodhoundbooks.com

www.ingramcontent.com/pod-product-compliance
Ingram Content Group UK Ltd.
Pitfield, Milton Keynes, MK11 3LW, UK
UKHW042003190726
13854UKWH00005B/2145

9 781916 978607